The Curse of the Goddess
Ratan Lal Basu

1

The Curse of the Goddess

Ratan Lal Basu

Published by Kautilya, 2023.

The Curse of the Goddess

© Author Ratan Lal Basu

Copyright 2023

This is a work of fiction. Similarities to real people, places, or events are entirely coincidental.

THE CURSE OF THE GODDESS

First edition. January 22, 2023.

Copyright © 2023 Ratan Lal Basu.

ISBN: 979-8215496244

Written by Ratan Lal Basu.

The Curse of the Goddess

Contents

The Curse of the Goddess

Chapter 1: The Nymph

A vast expanse opened up as soon as Nilanjan Roy alias Nil took a U-turn around the steep hill and the panoramic view below enchanted him. The narrow causeway had sloped down with continued bends and lost into the greenery enveloping the village at its upper end and tiny houses of the village below were visible through the crevices of the network of the pines and rhododendrons. The early morning fog had dissipated and ahead to the north the mighty peaks of the Kanchenjunga were now glistening in the sun

and the sky above was clear except the patches of sooty clouds floating aimlessly across. The dark nimbus was still hanging motionless at the bottom of the mountain that had risen straight up to the snowy peaks.

It is not likely to rain and the day would be a fine one, Nil thought.

When he had got up early at dawn all his mates at the trekkers' hut were fast asleep. All except Nil had gone to bed late, drinking and playing card games. Nil did not like to awake the cook boy who was still sleeping and lighting the kerosene stove he prepared a strong raw coffee. The foggy weather outside was charming and the coffee was invigorating. It was extremely cold and he put on a wind protecting jacket over the sweater and tucked with the collar of the jacket the back of the large cap he had bought from Darjeeling. He stepped out the lowly wooden door of the hut and closed it. A chilly breeze greeted him and he shivered as the coldness pierced through the thick walls of the sweater and the jacket. It could be near one or two degrees Celsius he guessed. It was all foggy outside and only the tops of the trees and the crests of the hills showed through the dense fog. Walking in this eerie ambience was enchanting and he started exploring the hills that were scattered picturesquely around the place. He took a causeway that had gone gently down to the north and the walk through the mystic fog exhilarated him. He had now walked for about an hour and gone way off from the hut. His companions were not likely to rise soon but a trip to the beautiful village may take several hours, especially the uphill return journey and by this time they would wake and would be worried about Nil. But he could still spend a few hours and return to the hut before they would wake. He could have a better view from the top of the barren hillock about two hundred meters ahead and even the peaks of Mount Everest to the west of Kanchenjunga might be visible

from the top. The hillock was not very high likely to be about hundred meters and it had a gentle slope. So

Nil decided to climb the hillock and proceeded toward the bottom of the hill.

Approaching the foot of the hillock Nil was disappointed to find the approach to the way up cut off by a small stream originating from a cascading spring from the heights. The stream was not more than twenty feet in width and it was shallow. He would have to cross it barefoot, and the water must be very cold and the mossy stones at the bed, slippery. He hesitated for a while and finally decided to have a try. He ought not to give up after getting so close. All of a sudden a chilly gust of wind alerted him and looking up he noticed the mid sky now invaded by the nimbus which was now inflating and spreading like an unfolding blanket and he apprehended it would rain in no time. He knew the hazards of being drenched in this cold weather and so he hastened to return.

It started drizzling and Nil tried to accelerate the pace of walking but could hardly move faster as the wind was coming from the direction of his movement. He stopped for a while for breath and was panicked to discover that the path he was walking along now was not the one to the hut and in haste he had lost way. He would have to move back and find out the way to the hut and that needed thinking in cool brain.

He, however, did not find any time to think and plan as it started snowing heavily making everything invisible around. He looked frantically for some shelter but none to be found in this barren hill. The hillside close to him was inclined outward and no nook could be found for shelter and the extreme coldness made him frantic. It would be wise to move downhill and whatever way he took he could somehow reach the village below, he thought. He accelerated pace and almost started running downhill. He suddenly skidded on stray pebbles and started rolling downhill. Fear of falling down into the gorge and death overpowered his sense of pain and freezing cold. Soon he lost sense.

Nil opened his eyes with efforts and everything appeared hazy at first. He felt languid and tried to recollect what had happened to him but reminiscences were all hazy and incoherent. He closed his eyes again and dozed for a while. Then again he opened his eyes and slowly his vision became clear as the tapestry covering his sight disappeared. He discovered himself on a wooden cot in a small room with slanted asbestos roofs, wooden walls and lowly glass windows through which the distant hills, vales and the clear sky were visible and he racked his brains to realize how he happened to be there, in the strange surroundings. He was covered with a heavy rough blanket but he felt the pinch of the cold weather on his bare face and head. He wore the cap which was lying by the pillow and drew it closer. He turned aside and looked into the inside of the room which had a small door at the right corner. A Lepcha boy of about twelve years with a shabby tattered coat and bare head was standing a few feet from his bedstead and looking indifferently out the glass window at the other side. His unclean round face was chapped at places and covered with specks and coagulated mucous.

Gradually the haziness of his memory disappeared and he could remember everything since the morning – his misadventure at dawn, the snow storm, his losing way and being senseless. But how come he happened to be here in the strange ambience? Did this boy rescue him and brought him over to this room? That was impossible he thought. The tiny boy could hardly carry his bulk. It must be someone else. May be it was the father of the boy or some older companion. He should ask the boy and get everything clear. His mates at the hut must be worried by now. They had to be informed somehow – by this boy or

his older companion. He looked out the other window and noticed far away below the roofs of some houses of the village peeping through the network of pines. So he was close to the village but must be at the outskirt, he guessed. He now felt hungry and thirsty.

'Hey', he called the boy with effort as weariness had almost choked his voice and his voice sounded like 'eh' which gave the boy a start and he promptly looked back and a sweet smile played on his chapped lips. He looked happy to find Nil regaining consciousness and hastened close to his bedstead and asked in a sweet effeminate tone, 'kasto chha daju?' (how do you feel my elder brother?)

With utmost efforts Nil cleared his voice and blurted out, 'ramro' (well). Then he asked the boy if he could get him some warm water for drink.

'Certainly', the boy replied with alacrity and his small but shining eyes revealed that he was intelligent. 'I may also prepare tea for you if you like.'

'Sure. Strong tea without milk, but get me some water first.'

The boy turned for the door and before he could reach the door a tall Lama in deep red robe, shaved head, large forehead and bright eyes appeared at the door and said in a heavy voice, 'how do you feel now young man?'

'Well, but languid.'

'Take spice tea and all your weariness would be gone.'

'Where am I now?'

'You are at my cottage at the outskirts of the village. The village downhill is only a few minutes'
walk.'

'Is it you who had rescued me from the deadly snowstorm and brought me over to this place?'

'No,' the Lama smiled affably, 'I rarely get out of this place. It's the blessed girl Doma who has rescued you. She has a divine power and can sense who is in danger around this place and promptly moves to the spot to rescue the victim.'

This gave Nil a start, a girl had rescued him. She must be strong. Is she beautiful? Nil queried himself.

Suppressing his sudden emotion Nil asked, 'where is she?'

'Gone out to inform your friends at the trekkers' hut and she's likely to return soon and I believe your friends would accompany her.'

'How did she know that I had been in the trekkers' hut?'

'Very easy. You're a Bengali from outside and all outsiders put up at the hut as there's no other place for the outsiders to stay here.'

The boy returned with a glass of water and Nil gulped it hurriedly. 'Need more?' The boy asked. 'No, you now get the tea,' Nil replied. The boy smiled affably and left.

'Okay take spice tea and biscuits and thereafter take rest till the girl returns.'

The Lama left and Nil's mind drifted aimlessly. 'How does the girl look? Must be pretty and charming.' A feeling of thrill coursed through him to think of the girl embracing and carrying his unconscious body. He turned toward the outer window close to his bedstead and looking out watched the valley lined with pines and rhododendrons and the distant hills looked deep blue with patches of white cloud stacked in the crevices and the snow plastering the crest scintillating in bright sunshine. There was no sign of the snowstorm in the clear sky, but the coldness was pinching. He drew down the cap and tightened the back close to the collar of his jacket and covered his head and face with the blanket keeping only the eyes outside. He was amazed to think of the fickleness of the weather here. 'Hills are always unpredictable like the young girls' Nil said to himself and was again thrilled to think of his rescuer. The umbrella like foliage of the large pine tree bending inward from the edge of the hill that had sloped steeply down to the valley, was swaying in the gentle breeze spreading in the air powdery spores that hung on the air for some time and floated down to dissipate slowly. The shorter pines were still covered with snow and looked like white umbrellas. His cot was small and there was a similar cot at the other end of the room and it was heaped with blankets and pillows and there were a few small stools and a small wooden table in the room. On the rope diagonally tied across the room were towels and red robes and on the wooden shelves jutting out of the walls were stacked heavy books. 'These may be sacred Buddhist texts' he thought. At the corner of the room there was a large statue of Buddha and the image of a grotesque goddess alongside. There were flowers at the feet of the deities and utensils of various designs and small instruments for worship. He had once seen them in a Tibetan museum at Gangtok.

'Daju cha.' (here's your tea elder brother).

Nil looked back and found the boy standing with a large porcelain cup and some biscuits. The boy pushed the table close to the bedstead and placed the cup and the plate of biscuits on it. The spice tea was a bit pungent but Nil liked it and got refreshed after a few gulps. The boy stood like a spring doll and watched him taking tea and biting the biscuits. The biscuits whetted his suppressed appetite and he felt morbidly hungry.

'Can you prepare some food for me? I feel very hungry.'

'We've only egg-noodles. Like it?'

'Why not?' Nil said in a lively tone, 'prepare it as early as possible. Hunger is biting my stomach.' The boy nodded and left. Nil was surprised to hear the vigor of his own voice which was choked only a few minutes ago. The spice tea had worked like magic, he thought.

Nil now looked again out the window at the distant hills and fragments of reminiscences started streaming relentlessly through his mind. He was drowsy now and in intermittent dozes odd dreams started drifting through his mind.

In the mystic world of his dreams he got transported back to his adolescence running across a lush green field, hand-in-hand with the neighboring girl Mili. All of a sudden the field turned into a barren hilly tract and Mili's face turned into that of a Lepcha girl and suddenly everything changed and he was with his college mates taking cold drinks from a Calcutta stall at College Street which again turned into a church and he was now alone stepping down a staircase into a dark pit and his legs skidded and he started

falling in the fathomless pit and his sleep broke and he was relieved to realize it was just a horrible dream, but he was perspiring even in this cold weather. He removed the blanket for a while to cool off.

Mili was his lone friend from the very childhood. After he got admitted to a Calcutta College Mili regularly wrote him mails and he replied promptly. In summer and puza vacations he used to return to his village and could meet Mili who was then studying at a local college. They used to meet under a tree at the bank of the river at the outskirt of the village and talked hours on end about their future. After he had passed the B. Sc. exam with first class he got admitted to the University of Calcutta but Mili was plucked

and her parents arranged for her marriage. Mili wrote him about her predicament as she was not willing to marry anybody else but Nil and requested him to come back immediately and convince her parents. He learnt from his mother that they may postpone the wedding only if they were assured that Nil would

marry Mili within two years. But how could he marry before he passed the last exam and got a job? He desired her no doubt but he had nothing to do at that moment. So he did not reply Mili and in disgust she consented to the arranged marriage, but later on he learn that she still loved him.

After Mili's marriage he lost interest in everything and his results of the M.Sc. exam was not satisfactory but fortunately he got a lecturer's job at a Calcutta college and he readily accepted it as with his results it was no longer possible to get a chance in the Ph. D. course in any US university and thus his long cherished dream was shattered.

Many girl students and some female colleagues wanted to be intimate with him, may be because of his extremely handsome appearance, but he always dissuaded them. Then he came upon a saffron clad

religious man and became his disciple. The man appeared very wise and Nil along with other disciples was highly impressed by his wisdom and he suggested Nil to be an ascetic and never to marry.

One day the man was arrested for stealing gold ornaments from a temple of goddess Kali. The police also interrogated and harassed Nil and other disciples of the fake religious man. Nil got completely disillusioned and frustrated. Then all of a sudden he came upon Mili again.

It was two months' summer vacation and Nil was touring various hill towns. At Simla he came upon Mili whose husband was then working at a private firm at the hill town and she had two children. She discovered him at a fancy goods stall. He at first could not recognize her as the lean girl had now become a robust full fledged lady. She called him aloud, 'hey Nil, you're here?'

Finding Nil glancing at her with bewildered eyes she giggled and in a moment he could recognize her and replied. 'I'm here to visit this hill town, but how come you're here?'.

Her eyes brightened and Nil's heart fluttered to find her devouring him with her glance. They explained to each other how they happened to be there and then she invited him to her husband's flat. It was not far off from the stall and after she had purchased porcelain tea cups and plates they proceeded on foot to her flat. They felt as though they had been back to their childhood days and both were ebullient and talkative. Her hubby was now in office and children at school. He sat in the large well decorated drawing room and she went inside to get changed and prepare coffee and some food for him. He told her to prepare coffee only as he had taken heavy breakfast only a few minutes ago. After twenty minutes she returned with the coffee. She was now only with a mini skirt and lingerie above hardly covering her huge boobs. Nil felt embarrassed to have an immediate hard on. As soon as he had finished the coffee she hugged him hard uttering madly, 'I love you Nil, I love you' and her tongue was inside his mouth in no time. Nil could not restrain himself.

He stayed at Simla for about two weeks and every night he felt moral prick and vowed not to meet her again but when she came to pick him up at noon he could not keep his vow. After return to Calcutta he was languishing in guilt consciousness. Soon he got a mail from Mili that she was missing him badly and coming to Calcutta very soon. He did not reply her and left Calcutta so that he was not again trapped into the vice. To avoid Mili permanently he sought a job outside Calcutta. The non-academic atmosphere at the college was also against his ethics. Nil started working as a freelance journalist and remained

outside Calcutta for some time. He completed his Ph. D. in the meantime. His guide introduced him with Rajib Mitra, a business man running several private educational institutes. He soon joined Mr. Mitra's institute.

From his very childhood he liked hill trekking and so when he learnt that some of the journalists known to him were going out for a trek at Sandhak-Fu hills he opted to join them.

'Your friends are coming. I've seen them at the turn of the road uphill and they'll be here in no time.' The voice of the boy drew Nil back from the past. He hesitated to ask if the girl was with them. He

wanted to get rid of Mili because of her overwhelming lust but he still loved her and could not forget her and no other girl, however beautiful, could attract him. But now he again felt spontaneous attraction for the Lepcha girl even before seeing her.

The boy told that he had seen them at the last bend where the causeway to this cottage was connected with the downhill track to the village. They were likely to come in about half an hour, Nil thought. The boy told that he had seen two men along with the mystic girl. The two men were for sure his fellow trekkers. His heart leapt up as the thought of the girl. 'How does she look? Could she be ugly? It is impossible', he thought. The way the Lama talked about her she ought to be beautiful. He could not hold himself. Half an hour seemed to be eternity. He sat up on the bed and felt his debility was gone. He was

no longer feeling chilly. The vital heat had returned. He could now go out and look for them.

'Help me out of bed', Nil requested. The boy promptly came close to his bed and extended his hand. No much effort was needed for him to get down the cot. He got his jacket and cap fastened tightly and felt comfortable. As he made for the door, the boy who was closely following him now said ecstatically,

'daju, you're perfectly fit now.' Nil came out of the room and stepped down the wooden stairs to the

small courtyard of the cottage. The distant hills now looked hazy as clouds were again gathering around the crests and moving slowly toward the mid sky. They were pure white cirrus different from the sooty ones that meant rain or snowfall. He noticed below three humanoid figures in the crevice between two clusters of pines in a flash and they disappeared again behind the thick pines. Now it could be a matter of ten minutes or thereabouts.

He stepped forward to the corner of the steep slope that went down straight up to the bend of the causeway leading to this place. He stood leaning against the pine that had taken a kinky bent into the slope of the hill and he watched the gentle breeze playing on the foliage spreading like an umbrella. The

entire path zigzagging up to the Lama's cottage was now distinctly visible and he discovered them turning the last bend and climbing the last part of the causeway about fifty feet away. He could recognize two of the fellow trekkers, Jibes Tribedi and Suresh Thawre and the girl was in a multi colored robe, a red ribbon fastening neatly her thick black hair and her round face was devastatingly pretty. Nil grabbed the pine trunk hard to restrain the trepidations of his heart. He felt terribly nervous. He could not make out how to initiate talks with her. He started constructing sentences and dismissing them and trying again. Then he heard the loud 'hello' form the two friends who rushed toward him and shook hands warmly. Doma stood close by with a charming smile in her lips and her eyes shining mystically.

'Oh, we feel relieved to see you perfectly well', Jibes said.

'We were really worried to learn about your condition from the hill girl, and did not waste a moment to start for this place', Suresh said panting, as the uphill journey had already made him breathless.

'You better get inside and talk,' Doma said in a sweet voice and they made for the cottage and Nil felt with relief that the company of the friends had helped him overcome the nervousness and he told Doma in a normal voice, 'I don't find any words to thank you for saving my life.'

Doma said politely, 'you need not thank me; it's not me but God who hath saved your life.'

The three of them were served with spice tea and locally made biscuits. Doma came into the room and shrugging off all his nervousness Nil inquired about how she had found and rescued him. She displayed a sweet smile, squinted and a mystic glint played in her small but beautiful eyes. She slowly unraveled the entire incident with minute details. Snowfall had a special attraction for her since her very childhood and she liked waltzing under snowfall. This day too she was exhilarated as snowfall started all of a sudden without any prior indication. She was then gossiping with her brother and sisters. She immediately got dressed up in warm clothes and with her large umbrella went out into the snow and she had to open the umbrella to protect her head as the snow was now falling in hard beads. She started singing and dancing in tune with the ringing noise made by the beads as they struck the hard rocks. Suddenly her sixth sense gave an alarm and she felt someone must be in danger. This queer feeling used to come from the depth of her mind if somebody in this hill region was ever in danger, and nobody could

explain this supernatural faculty of Doma. The Lamas and the monks explained this to be a rare gift of the god, she being the favored and blessed one. This caused her much embarrassment as everyone revered her and considered her different from them. She felt her special power only if somebody was in danger. Otherwise she was an ordinary girl but nobody would believe her and considered her to be a heavenly nymph born as a human.

Like her earlier experiences, this time too, Doma went into sort of trance, moved ahead like an automaton being driven by some unknown force beyond her control and reaching at the spot she was panicked to find Nil lying prostrate like a corpse, snow beads lashing him mercilessly. She held her hand to his nostrils and was relieved to find him still breathing though mildly. She immediately lifted him on her back and by instinct his hands entwined her neck. Holding his hands tight on her chest by one hand and the umbrella by the other, she proceeded toward the village cautiously as any false step could be fatal.

The eyes of the two friends got enlarged to hear about the strength and prowess of the girl and blood rushed to Nil's head to visualize himself on her back entwining her neck and his hands resting on her chest.

Coming near the Lama's cottage, she thought it would be wiser to carry him to the cottage as the village was far down and she could not waste time considering his precarious condition. Moreover she also felt a bit tired after carrying his bulk to this distance. The approach to the hut was a steep rise and coming to the bend from where the causeway had emerged, she called aloud the boy and seeing her both the boy and the Lama climbed down and helped her carry Nil into the outer room of the cottage. Laying him on the cot the Lama loosened his garments, covered him with heavy blankets and examined his breathing and eyes. The Lama immediately held to his nostrils an herbal medicine for inhaling till his breathing became normal and thereafter forced open his mouth and dropped some powder on Nil's tongue. He assured Doma, 'don't worry, the danger is over now. He would recover in half an hour. There's no doubt this Bengali young man is a trekker and you may find his mates at the government trekkers' hut. In case they are out trekking drop the word to the caretaker or attendants. So hurry up and go to the hut; his mates might be worried over his delay in returning.'

Doma immediately started for the trekkers' hut. It was good luck that the trekkers had taken it as a rest day and all of them were in the hut. Learning about the incident, Jibes and Suresh immediately got ready to accompany her to the Lama's cottage.

Nil and his two friends thanked her for saving Nil's life and she with a sweet smile said, 'it's not me but God who hath saved his life. In fact, I was forced to do this by the power of God which had nestled in me for the time being.' The Lama supported the view of Doma and explained that everything in our lives happen by the will of God and we are but playthings at the hands of the almighty.

The girl now looked intently at Nil's forehead and asked how he had got the trident mark on his forehead. Nil smiled and said that he had this since his birth and it was a mystery to everybody and there had been many explanations so far, but the rational ones opined that this was but a freak of nature. The girl called the Lama and showed him the sign and talked for a while in a local dialect. The Lama started nodding his head again and again and Nil and his friends realized that they were talking about the sign on his forehead but could not understand what they were talking. However, their gestures assured them that there was nothing mischievous about the sign. While asked the Lama said, 'this is the sign of Lord Shiva and a very sacred sign for a Hindu. We're in some problem and he with this auspicious mark may be of some help. I'll explain this to you later on.'

Before they left Doma once again had some talks in their dialect with the Lama and asked them,

'what is your trekking schedule for tomorrow, would you leave the hut early?'

'As we are all very tired we've decided to trek some small hills tomorrow and would leave the hut late, say at about 11 a.m.', Jibes replied.

'When would you return to Calcutta?'

'We'll trek three more days and thereafter leave for New Jalpaiguri from where by train to Calcutta.'

'Okay, tomorrow I'll visit your hut long before your trekking starts.'

His friends asked Nil again if he was in a condition to undertake the troublesome uphill journey to the hut. He felt now perfectly well and responded smiling, 'it would be no problem.'

'In case he feels uncomfortable on the way don't hesitate to return and the girl would later on accompany him to the hut whenever he is completely fit,' the Lama reminded them.

All the way to the hut Nil remained obsessed with the thought of Doma, her shining eyes, sweet accent of speaking Hindi and also of her talks with the Lama about the trident sign on his forehead. He responded laconically to the queries of his friends who, thinking him to be exhausted because of the horrible experience, decided not to disturb him. They started hollering and exclaiming as new views opened up in every turn of the zigzag track.

It was almost dark when they reached the hut. All the trekkers were relieved to find Nil perfectly fit and in vigorous health. They had already seen Nil and his two companions from a distance and ordered

the cook to prepare momos and coffee. Nil was now terribly hungry and devoured a lot of momos and two cups of strong coffee without milk and sugar. The porters and the guide assembled around them and looked at Nil with deep reverence, he being the blessed one to get the help of the divine girl. They had strong belief that everything was ordained by god to get him acquainted with the nymph who was known and revered by every hill people around the place. Nil's inadvertent venture, being in danger and being

rescued by the girl, all were pre-arranged by god. Their belief was strengthened when Nil told about the interest of Doma and the Lama in his trident mark and their desire to seek his help to resolve a problem.

The guide told Nil and his trekker friends the legends about the girl who, according a Nepali Hindu monk, had been an apsara dancer (celestial nymph) in the court of Lord Indra, the king of the Hindu gods. In the heaven she had seduced the husband of a powerful goddess and the angry goddess cursed her to be born as a human being. After her birth as a Buddhist Lepcha girl, she prayed to Lord Buddha, who blessed her with the assurance that if she could perform some pious deeds she would be free from the curse and would once again return to the court of Indra. The Lord now had made arrangements to facilitate her

pious deeds and they believed Nil was a part of that divine design.

Nil could not sleep well that night and dozed with mysterious dreams. His mind was preoccupied with the myths of Doma and his miraculous involvement with her and the problem of the Lepchas.

In his dream he found himself in a vast flat ground by the side of a half frozen lake encircled by snow covered lofty peaks. He realized it was the Kailas mountain and the lake was Manas Sarovar, the abode of Lord Shiva. He was in god's attire, the garments sequined with scintillating gold threads. His large crown was adorned with diamonds, rubies, emeralds and other gems. He was ushered by the horned Nandi god into the foggy place and found Lord Shiva in deep meditation and an apsara prostrating at his feet. The apsara was none but the Lepcha girl Doma. He wanted to move forward to reach near her but being pushed by Nandi god he fell on the snow and started rolling down and his sleep broke. He again fell into doze and now he was racing after a girl in a vast barren field mystified with a mellow blue light. The face of the girl interchanged between Mili's and Doma's. The distance between them got shortened and as soon as he tried to touch her, she vanished and reappeared at a distance beckoning Nil. He again got

closer and the girl vanished again and his sleep broke. Next time he discovered himself in a semi-dark cave, amidst horrible ghosts. The ghosts started closing in with clenched teeth and he shrieked out loudly. The trekker nearest to him asked, 'what happened?' Then he came over to Nil's bed and removed his hands from his chest and said, 'don't sleep on your back with your hands on the chest.'

Nil blubbered out in sleepy voice, 'sorry for disturbing your sleep.' He turned to the side but could not sleep for the rest of the night. Next morning all the trekkers got up early and started packing up necessary things for the day's trek. The guide started giving instructions showing the map of the hills to be trekked. Doma came at 9 a.m. and got right to business,

'we are in a fix and we seek Nil's help. The Lama is willing to talk with him about the matter. Can you please spare him if, of course, he is willing to help us postponing trekking? We'd arrange for his return and he would join you at New Jalpaiguri on the day of your departure.'

'We've no problem if Nil himself is willing', the leader of the team replied.

'Gladly', Nil replied promptly and he looked ecstatic.

'But don't fail to reach New Jalpaiguri on time', the leader reminded Nil. Nil bade good bye to his friends and proceeded for the village with Doma.

Chapter 2: The Curse

The sky was cloudy and the sun had not yet shown its face. Nil felt chilly at first but after a few minutes' walk he felt warm and sweating inside the jacket. As he wanted to put off the jacket Doma forbade, 'don't do this, soon there would be chilly wind and you'll catch cold.' It was about ten but the clouds overhead had made the ambience semi dark. 'It may start raining at any moment', Nil expressed apprehension and Doma showed him two large umbrellas in reply. The fine layer of cloud climbing down the crest of the hills toward the valley downhill looked like a off-white smooth blanket and nothing below could be visible. After the initial uphill journey the downhill walk was now comfortable but Doma

warned, 'walk cautiously, lest you should step on pebbles or rock fragments and....' she raised her fingers in a funny way toward the sky and made a peculiar gesture that made Nil laugh loudly. Doma giggled and started humming a sweet song in an unknown language. She looked very elated.

As soon as they started climbing the causeway leading to the Lama's cottage, the boy noticed them from above and informed the Lama and raced down the path to greet them, 'daju, you're now perfectly well.' They waited there for some time and were entertained with spice tea. The Lama soon came down to business,

'we are in a grave problem and we have been looking vainly for the right person, the lone pious Hindu with a trident mark on his forehead. Now by God's grace you're here. You yourself don't know who you are, but your auspicious sign shows that you are the man sent on earth by Lord Shiva to rescue us. Now can you take a little trouble to help us out of a grave crisis?'

'I myself don't have any trust on my divinity, but accepting your conviction I'm ready to help you my best, but at present I've important preoccupations at Calcutta and I must return with the trekkers.'

'You need not help us right now. Return to Calcutta now and our men would contact you in time.'

'But what is the problem?'

'You go with this girl down to the village. They have arranged for your accommodation there and you would learn in detail about the problem from this girl and her father and thereafter I'll talk with you once again before you depart.'

Nil proceed for the village with Doma and was obsessed with deep thought all the way. He was really puzzled to learn about his divine power which he himself was unaware of.

As soon as they reached the village a large number of villagers including children came forward to welcome Nil. He was presented with flowers and garlands. All of them followed them up to the house of Doma. They had deep respect for Hindu Bengalis who rarely visited this village which was excluded from the map for the tourists and trekkers. Doma had already informed them that a Bengali globe trotter would visit the village and reside there for some time. The Lama had directed that none of the villagers except Doma and her parents should have any inkling of Nil's real purpose of visit.

Yalmo Lepcha, the father of Doma, a robust and short man around forty five with a large round face, small eyes and a curved goatee on the chin, cordially received Nil and took him right inside the house where Doma's mother, greeted him with a simple smile. Doma's lone brother Yaneda and two sisters, Risika and Susma assembled around him and the little girl of four Susma started examining his jacket and was rebuked by her mother. Nil told her not to chide the sweet child and lifted her right up to his lap. Her mother laughed and said, 'you don't know sir how naughty she is!' He felt hungry and his meal, thupka and curry of beans was served soon and as he was not willing to take any alcoholic drinks, he was given fruit wine with mild alcoholic content and he relished the sweet-sour taste of the beverage. It was a two storey house and the upper floor opened up to the road above, the same road that had turned uphill from the door of the ground floor. He took some rest and fell asleep as he was very tired of the tedious journey.

His sleep broke in the afternoon and it was now raining in cats and dogs. He was to put up at the vacant house of a businessman, but because of the rain they could not move out. Doma told her father, 'if the rain do not subside soon we'll have to arrange for his night halt in our house.'

She turned toward Nil and said, 'it may be uncomfortable for you to stay here with so many family members, but nothing else could be done if the rain continues.'

Nil replied in an ecstatic tone, 'that would be fine. I'd be happy to stay here with your family members. In fact I wanted to propose staying here at the very moment I'd arrived here as I felt uneasy to spend the night alone in a desolate house but hesitated to tell you considering problem of your family. How far is the vacant house, by the way?'

'About half a mile uphill, a very beautiful place.'

'Why do you take so much trouble to accommodate me there? You'll have to carry food to that distance. I may go on staying here if you have no problems on your part.'

At this both her parents said happily, 'oh that would be very nice; we would have no problem at all. We were only thinking about your problem with the strangers.'

'You are no longer strangers to me,' Nil said seriously.

The rain subsided in the evening and stars were visible in the clear sky. Being at a much lower altitude this place was not very cold. Doma went out to meet the Lama once again. Her brother and sisters

took him out over to a point from where all the hills and valleys around could be seen, but now in the darkness only scattered dots of light were visible from all sides and above and the dark crests of the hills looked like gigantic heads of demons. The dots of lights, as though adorning the dark swaying pines, appeared like fire flies roaming around.

They were eager to tell him ghost stories. The atmosphere, the dark canvas embroidered with dots of lights and the dark wood under the starry sky made the ambience appropriate for horror stories. The brother of the girl, a boy of fifteen, told that before their birth, his father was the first man to build his house here. He had a dispute with his parents about his marriage, their mother being a Hindu Nepali girl. So his parents married secretly and left the Rimbik town to get settled here. Then only a few residents lived in this Lepcha village and their house was then at an isolated place about two miles uphill from the cluster of houses of the twenty residents of the small village. His father had bought this plot very cheap from a Bhutia transport operator.

Both his parents were very hardy and they did not interfere in the religious practices of each other – his father was a worshipper of Lord Buddha, and his mother of Shiva. They lived happily, with the earning from their grocery shop at the village downhill. Their mother also used to sew cotton bags at home and mostly remained home. Yalmo, their father looked after the shop with the help of two working

hands from the village and every weekend he used to go to the nearest town to buy wares for his shop and sell the bags made by their mother. He used to return from the shop in the evening. That day he was late because there was a dance and music program in the house of a villager. He was returning home at about ten p.m. It was a new moon night and the sky was starry. Approaching near the house he stopped short to notice a tiny ball of green light dropping down from the sky. The light dot became larger and larger and it looked like a round craft. The craft slowly nestled on the hillock that rose from the gorge below and a side door opened up. He was utterly panicked and hastened into the house and knocked at the door heavily. Their mother opened the door and asked what had happened. He went inside and asked her to close the door. Going upstairs he showed her the craft through the glass window. Now a few humanoid figures, looking like robots, had come down on the hilltop and roaming leisurely around. They got panicked and started praying to their deities. The extra terrestrial men stayed there for a few minutes and then entered the vehicle which left after making a hissing noise and disappeared into the sky.

The next day they found that all the trees on the hillock were charred. and the rock at the top had got flattened and polished like marble. When Yalmo related the incident to the villagers the elderly ones told that the vehicle was from another planet far away from the earth and others too had seen it in earlier times. Nobody could tell what they landed there for. But each time they came some misfortune befell the locality. This time too there was an unknown disease in which all the poultry of the villagers were killed. Their mother had got panicked and asked his father to change their residence and get settled inside the village, but the elderly people said that these creatures never land to the same spot twice. The year after the incident their elder sister was born and she displayed supernatural power and everybody opined that

the birth of the auspicious child had got something to do with the landing of the extra terrestrial creatures. These landings do not always bring misfortune alone. There were evidence of good luck accompanying their mysterious visits.

Being asked to tell his story Nil started the Dracula story and he had to stop as Susma got panicked and insisted on returning home. Nil went back to the house with them and started telling them interesting animal stories. In the mean time Doma returned and was very glad to find Nil getting on well with the children. While he asked her about the landing of the vehicle, she and her father told that the story was true and their recent misfortune had something to do with the latest landing of it on the upper hill.

'Have your dinner first and I'll tell you about the entire incident,' Yalmo insisted. Nil took his dinner with haste being eager to learn about the incident.

The house had three rooms at the ground floor and two at the first, one bed room and the other for dining. After dinner all the family members except Yalmo were accommodated at the ground floor and the latter with Nil at the first floor. Doma's mother and the children bade him goodnight. Yalmo and Doma entered his room and got seated on two stools close to Nil's bed on which Nil, in a reclining

position, waited patiently for the account of the mysterious incident. Yalmo pursed his lips, dropped some cloves in his mouth and started the story.

'For a few years after I had seen the vehicle, nobody heard any incident of landing of any extra- terrestrial vehicle. Then it appeared again when Doma was about six year old and Yaneda was just born. Some new houses were then built in this place and the place was no longer lonely. One midnight I was awakened by the hollering of a neighboring boy and hearing the 'bip bip' sound I, Doma and her mother got on to the roof with palpitating hearts and noticed the uncanny vehicle with bluish glow slowly gliding down the sky toward the high hilltop to the north. Many of my neighbors were also watching the spectacle with awe stricken eyes. The vehicle had almost touched the ground when a sharp explosion deafened us and the rumbling sent tremors across the hills and vales as though by an earthquake. Then the forest, surrounding the hilltop, was ablaze, the flames rising high up into the sky. The conflagration continued

for several days and when it subsided the entire forest at the crest was burnt to ashes.

All the hill people fell silent and we waited for the misfortune to follow the horrible incident. Suddenly we were relieved as a sacred looking tantric, from Tarapith near Calcutta, visited the village and assured us that by his tantric power he would save us from the curse that was likely to befall us in no time.

The tantric told us that he had learnt about the incident through meditation. He then unraveled the mystery of the heavenly vehicle which belonged to goddess Kali. Long ago, when nobody lived in these hills a Buddhist tantric from Tibet had selected this site for his occult practices and the goddess Kali used to communicate with him through the heavenly vehicle. He achieved the highest stage of meditation and Nirvana. But after his direct transportation to divine land, the vehicle still used to visit this place occasionally. The curse associated with the arrival of the vehicle began after some misguided hill youths made fun of the nudity of the goddess Kali. The conflagration indicated that the misfortune this time would be the greatest and might annihilate all of us unless preventive measures were taken.

The tantric along with his disciples visited the burnt hilltop and assured us that he was capable of appeasing the goddess and rescuing us from the curse. He went back and returned after a few days with

his Nepali disciples with some instruments that he told would be necessary to erect a statue of the goddess at the approach of the cursed hilltop and he, through worship of the goddess and mantras would create a protective barrier at the border so that no evil force could escape to take possession of our lives.

Soon a vast statue of the goddess was erected at the approach of the burnt hilltop which was in fact a fat plateau. All the hill people were invited to the first gorgeous puza of the goddess.

The tantric forbade us to trespass into the cursed land. This time nothing ominous happened and this increased our trust on the tantric. We offered goats for sacrifice at the altar of the goddess whenever the tantric asked for. We visited the image occasionally but never trespassed into the cursed plateau. One year passed without any trouble and in the meantime a beautiful temple was built around the image of the goddess. Trouble started because of the inadvertence of two naughty boys. Two boys of the village were missing and the tantric's men informed us that the boys had inadvertently entered the cursed land and

were killed by the dakinis (the female guards of goddess Kali). The tantric also expressed apprehensions that we too would not be spared this time as the entry of the boys had weakened the protective wall. He, however, did his best to repair the protective barrier but all in vain.

The water of the perennial spring coming down from the northern hills dried up soon after the incident and we were in grave trouble. We could somehow manage to collect water for drinking and other domestic uses from a spring a few kilo meters downhill but shortage of irrigation water destroyed our vegetable cultivation during winter and spring and the families dependent on cultivation alone were in grave financial trouble.

We then approached the tantric again and sought his help. The tantric told us that it was beyond is power to remove the curse fully at that moment but it could be temporarily removed if we abide by his directions. In between two rainy seasons when there is acute water crisis in the village we should send a few laborers for the service of the goddess and it is likely to lessen the curse temporarily and resume flow of water in the spring for a few hours. But he did not know yet if it would work but he might give a try.

Since then during each dry season we have been sending laborers to the tantric. They have to perform some secret tasks for the tantric. The experience of all of them is the same. None could remember

anything during their stay in the cursed land. The flow of water resumes during the stay of the laborers on the plateau, but the flow is intermittent and duration of each flow is very short. This is quite inadequate to meet the irrigation requirements during the dry seasons. When we related the problem to the tantric he informed us that anything more is beyond his power at the moment but he assured that he had learnt through meditation that the situation is likely to improve and the curse completely removed in a few years if we stick to our promise and never violate any norms set by him. But the poor cultivators could hardly wait that long. So we looked for some alternative although we still had trust on the power of the tantric.

We soon learnt about a very old Hindu sage with supernatural power residing at a cave in Nepal. I and a few other elderly villagers met the sage. We had to wait for a few days as the sage remains silent except on Sundays. Finding us after opening his eyes, the sage told that he was already well aware of our problem, but unfortunately the solution was beyond his power and probably no one except a pious young Hindu with a trident mark on his forehead would be able to rescue us from the curse. Since then we have been frantically looking for the pious man at all conceivable places but all our efforts have so far been fruitless. Now by accident we have discovered you, the pious Hindu as described by the Nepali ascetic.'

Nil felt embarrassed to hear all these and protested, 'I'm an ordinary man without any religious practice and how can I remove the curse, where great tantrics and sages have failed?'

Yalmo said calmly, 'but you're the right man although you yourself may not be aware of the dormant divine power in you.'

'But I don't know what I'm to do and moreover, I'm to leave for Calcutta on an urgent assignment the day after tomorrow.'

'We too do not have any idea about the way you're likely to help us. We are to learn this from the old sage at Nepal. You may now return to Calcutta and we'll contact you in time.'

After going to bed Nil's head was filled with torrents of confusing thoughts. It seemed dubious to him if he had really any such divine power and he could be of any help at all to the villagers to save them from the curse. His trident mark was simply an accidental birth mark, like large moles and black patches on the body of a child. Suddenly from the very depth of his memory, an incident came alive. He was then about five years old. He had gone to visit Banaras with his parents.

While they were coming out of the Viswanath temple a saffron clad elderly monk came forward and grabbing his hand started glancing at his forehead intently. At this his father burst into rage and ordered the monk in a grave voice, 'let go of my son's hand immediately.'

The monk looked at Nil's father calmly, 'yes babu, I should have sought your permission before grabbing his hand, but noticing the auspicious mark on his forehead I got so much excited that I could not hold myself. Forgive me babu, but I must tell you that you're lucky. Your son is not an ordinary person but has born with some divine power.'

His father laughed out loudly and said 'stop all nonsense' and then in Hindi, 'why are you wasting time by going the roundabout way? Tell me frankly if you need some money and I'd give it gladly.'

The monk squinted and his face was filled with a charming smile and he said politely, 'man, you

have mistaken me to be a fake sadhu. I am a resident and teacher of a Vedanta ashram at Rishikesh. There is no exaggeration in what I've said about your son.'

'Okay, thank you for your compliments', Nil's father said impatiently and pulling at Nil's hand started away from the sadhu. Nil's mother got infuriated and snatching out Nil from his father's hand and led him again to the sadhu who was about to leave the place as a large number of curious people had gathered around him. She offered pranam to the sadhu and made Nil do so and said entreatingly, 'Maharaj bless my son.' The sadhu raised his hand for blessings and said, 'Ma, I'm blessing him formally just for your satisfaction, but he has already been the blessed one of Lord Shiva who has left the mark of his trident on his forehead.'

His father laughed away what the sadhu had said but his mother still believed that Nil had some supernatural power which would be revealed one day. Now was this the time for his power to blossom? Nil still felt doubtful about all these mysteries surrounding his trident mark.

He fell asleep and soon got into the land of dreams.

He dreamt of walking barefoot across a vast ground under the starry sky in the new moon night. On both sides of the dusty track were grotesque tantrics in red robes meditating with skulls on tiger skins in the mellow light of the sacred ovens. Some of the tantrics eyed him with curiosity but nobody said him anything nor did anyone object to his trespassing into the territory meant for the tantrics alone. He now had gone far ahead where the place was lonely and no more tantrics were in sight. He heard some hushed voices from the undulating land ahead and he was terrified to see skulls and bony arms floating in the air only a few feet from him.. Someone called him from behind and looking back he noticed a group of

tantrics running toward him. They came close to him and said, 'don't go any further ahead into the land of the ghosts and you'd fall dead the moment you step into the forbidden territory.' A tantric came forward and extended his hand to grab him, but as soon as he reached near Nil a ray came out of his forehead and the tantric was thrown a few feet away. The eldest tantric now came close to him and looked closely at his forehead and said to his companions, 'he's not an ordinary man like us; he's protected by Lord Shiva and no evil spirits can do him any harm.' Then he told Nil, 'you must be a divine man and go ahead with your mission.' Then they offered him pranam with folded hands and vanished. Nil moved forward as though dragged by some force beyond his control and all of a sudden the sky became cloudy and nothing ahead could be visible. He could now hear only the hushed voices all around him and then he found him in front of a vast statue of goddess Kali. He soon realized it was not a statue but the live goddess herself. He fell at her feet and the goddess put her hand on his head and said affectionately, 'son you're the blessed one of my husband and you would be successful in your mission to help the hill people; but it would not be an easy task.. You would have to go through many hazards endangering your life, but through courage, patience, perseverance and intelligence you could be able to achieve your goal at the end and in your mission you should always keep with you the blessed Lepcha girl without whose help nothing could be achieved.'

Nil's sleep broke suddenly and he could not understand the meaning of the dream and thought it
could be the reflections of his own confused thoughts. He fell asleep again and it was a deep sleep without any dreams.

The next morning, his sleep broke as sunshine greeted him through the glass of the window and looking out he could not move his eyes from the fantastic view that was unfolding. He looked at the watch and leapt out of bed as it was about ten thirty. 'Oh, I've slept for such a long time,' he said to himself. He hastened to open the door and found the brother and sisters of Doma standing near the sill and smiling affably.

'I was going to knock at the door right now,' the brother said politely.

'You could have done it earlier; it has already been late', Nil said with worry.

Their mother came forward and asked affectionately, 'like to have your breakfast now?'.

'Oh sure, I'm awfully hungry, but I'm to finish my toilet chores first. Okay I'm getting ready in a few minutes. But where is Doma?'

'She has just gone out to talk with the Lama at his cottage and likely to return soon.'

Yalmo who was listening to their talks standing in the garden said, 'if you like to bathe I may get you warm water in a no time.'

'No need right now. I'll tell you if I need it tomorrow. In this cold weather I may as well go without baths for days', Nil said smiling.

Nil now went out with the tooth brush in his mouth and looked at the house from the hind side out of the ground floor and the house amidst the pines and rhododendrons looked picturesque. The sky was clear with small patches of cloud drifting across and the cluster of trees at the slopes of the distant hills looked like a chess board as sun rays could reach only the clusters projected outward, the inward ones remaining in the shadow.

The breakfast was bread and butter along with locally made alubakra jelly and the sweetish peach wine again. Doma returned soon and told that the Lama had some important works now and he would talk with Nil in the afternoon. She asked Nil if he would like to visit the village now and Nil readily gave consent. Doma got ready in a few minutes and went out with him for a visit of the village. Her brother and sisters were gloomy as their mother did now permit them to accompany Nil and Doma lest they create troubles. Doma led Nil across the village and showed him various places of interest. The village, surrounded by hills on all sides, looked like a cauldron. The hills were thickly covered with green pines and cryptomarius. A rivulet had gone through the entire length of the village like a serpent, but its bed

was dry and overgrown with grass and weeds.

There were about hundred Buddhist Lepcha families in the village, most of whom were peasants and they used to grow all sorts of vegetables, cabbages, cauliflowers, beans, beets, gourds, cucumbers, peas, radishes, red potatoes, carrots etc. The lush green of the vegetable fields, adorning the lower slopes of the hills and the spaces between the huts, were enchanting in the past, Doma said with nostalgic recollections. Produces of the fields over and above family needs were sold to urban markets, and with this income, necessaries from the towns were bought. But everything had changed now with the rivulet drying out by the curse of the goddess. The fields were dry now with sickly crops. She told that the tiny villages around were connected with each other by narrow hilly tracks cut at places by streams which had to be crossed along tree or rope bridges. The monastery was situated at a desolate valley beyond the hills to the south and they would have to cross a gorge over a rope bridge to reach the place.

Doma asked, 'do you like to visit the monastery?'

'Not now. Better let's go to the hilltop to the north and have glimpse of the cursed plateau.'

'Okay, but I don't like to stay there for a long time. The ominous plateau frightens me.'

On their way many local villagers were looking at Nil with curiosity and children with smiling faces greeted Nil and Doma. If anyone asked about the purpose of Nil's visit she told them that Nil was a tourist interested in visiting the remote hill villages. Doma once again cautioned Nil that his mission should be kept a strict secret; only she, her parents and the Lama would know it. If common villagers learnt about

the mission this would soon reach the knowledge of the tantric who would think that the Lepchas had lost confidence in him and appointed someone else to resolve their problem and he might be aggrieved and leave them completely unprotected against the curse. At present, whatever help he was providing by his capability was necessary and if he refrained from his protective worships, the task of Nil would become more difficult.

The track leading to the foothill had a gentle slope and Nil could not feel at all that he had already climbed about thousand feet. Now the village was visible like one in a satellite map. The dry water course further to the east was now clearly visible. It had come down like a snake and the lower reaches were overgrown with thick weeds that needed scanty water to live. The upper reach had turned behind a hill spreading eastward.

The hill, about thousand feet in altitude, was very steep, but there were thick pinewoods all the way and they could climb up easily by holding the trunks and branches of the pines and taking rest whenever necessary. Anticipating that their tour would take time, Doma had brought along their lunch packets and they had their lunch at a flat place just beneath the crest of the hill.

After lunch they started climbing the last twenty feet to the summit. This part was very steep and without any trees to hold on to. There were cracks on the rock body and Nil had to crawl to avert the risk of slipping down. Doma, however, was scaling the steep rise like a squirrel and finding Nil falling behind and struggling, she came down and extended her hand and caught hold of Nil's hand firmly. The touch of her strong but soft hand sent tremors down his spine. Doma did not feel any difficulty to drag Nil along and reaching the summit she let go of Nil's hand and burst into wild laughter that echoed back from the surrounding hills. She was now standing five feet from Nil, her body gesticulating with her laughter and the untied long hair floating wildly in the roaring wind. She now appeared like a heavenly nymph and Nil thought this too could be a dream. He was amazed and thrilled to think of being alone in an unknown land with a nymph. The barren hilltop was a circular space about fifteen feet in radius. All sides of the hill that

stood like a pyramid were covered with forests and curved into the other hills around. The curve to the north was the largest and it had a flat bottom after which it had sloped gently into a larger hill with a barren plateau at the top and Nil could understand that this was the cursed plateau. To the south east corner of the plateau the dome of the Kali temple of the tantric was glistening in sunshine. Doma now looked a bit panicked and entreated Nil not to look much at the cursed place and whispered in his ears,

'let's leave the place at once.'

While climbing down the barren part of the slope Nil took hold of Doma's arm and again he felt thrilled and also nervous.

Returning home they had snacks and tea and after an hour's rest they proceeded for the Lama's cottage. Now Yalmo too accompanied them. The Lama greeted them warmly and ushered them into the outer room. After tea, the Lama moved toward the door at the far corner of the room and signaled them to follow him. He instructed the boy to stand guard at the entrance of the cottage and to inform all visitors that the he was busy meditating and could not meet anyone before the next morning. The door opened

into a flight of stairs climbing down into a stuffy room closed on all sides by stone walls except the door at the bottom of the staircase. The Lama closed the door and got seated on a blanket spread over a raised square platform of stone at the middle of the room and requested them to sit down.

Nil guessed that the cellar was cut into the hill and was like a cave and in the semi darkness, with only a few dim candles at the feet of an antique Buddha statue cut into the stonewall, an eerie sensation coursed through Nil.

The Lama broke the silence, 'I've pondered over the matter very seriously and consulted some tantra books. No doubt Nil is the man to resolve our problem. But I'm still in the dark how he could be utilized.' He turned toward Nil and said, 'you go back to Calcutta. I'll soon visit the great Hindu sage at Nepal

and consult him and in accordance with his advice chalk out the mission for you and you would be informed in time.'

'After he comes to this place again and the mission explained to him' the Lama continued, 'we would have to wait for the auspicious moment to initiate the mission. Remember that this is a very secret

mission. Only me, Nil, Yalmo and Doma would know it. The tantric should not get any inkling that we've lost confidence in his capabilities.'

The Lama admitted that he had very little knowledge of the great mother goddess Kali revered by both the Hindus and the Bazrajan Buddhists and she is the goddess from which tantric power emerges. He asked Nil if he had any idea about the reason of her horrible appearance, her nudity, the garland of skulls entwining her neck and her blood thirsty protruding tongue.

It was now too late to return to their home and they decided to spend the night at the cottage and accordingly the Lama instructed the boy to prepare meals for the three guests. Nil started his story and resumed it after dinner.

'According to the Hindu puranas the ubiquitous, omnipotent, attribute-less Brahman desired to create the palpable universe and it was created by his will. As it was created out of nothingness it had to contain equal amounts of good and evil. These opposite attributes are present in every matter and particle of the universe. In the arena of the celestial beings, gods with nobler attributes and demons with baser attributes are opposed to each other, the gods living in the heaven and the demons in the Netherlands.

But at times intelligent demons perform painstaking meditations and are rewarded by the supreme gods like Brahma and Shiva. This makes the blessed demons much powerful to vanquish heaven driving out the gods who are compelled to take shelter with Lord Vishnu and Shiva. In such adverse circumstances Lord Vishnu advises the minor gods to invoke the root of all power, the mother goddess

Parvati who alone is capable of killing the demons. Parvati, the supreme goddess and source of all powers is also the cohort of Lord Shiva.

In her mission once Parvati was confronted with a demon called Raktabiz. The demon had the blessings of the supreme gods that if a single drop of his blood fell on the ground, hundred such demons would emerge out of it. So, Parvati was in serious trouble in course of her war with Raktabiz. Within a short time thousands of demons emerged out of the blood drops of the demons that were killed by the

goddess. She then invoked the goddess Kali who resided within her and Kali emerged from her forehead. Kali, being the most terrible aspect of the supreme mother power, went into a mad spree, slaughtering demons and drinking their blood which could not go beyond her protruding large tongue. She went on dancing and rejoicing the slaughter of the demons and made merriment by garlanding herself with the cut off heads of the demons.

Soon all the demons were killed but the goddess had gone into frenzy, even unaware that her garments had fallen down from her body making her completely nude. She still went on with her horrible cosmic dance shaking the entire universe. Realizing that the universe would soon collapse unless the goddess was restrained, everyone in the universe prayed to Lord Shiva who alone could restrain the crazy goddess. Shiva knew that no words or prayers would be able to restore her to senses. So he cunningly devised a way out. He lay on his back on her path and she being in a state of frenzy stepped on his chest and her instinct made her look down and being extremely perturbed to find herself setting feet on her husband's body which was a sin according to Hindu religion. She stopped her dance and was in a fix what to do and then she discovered that she was completely nude. Out of utter embarrassment she ran away and the universe was saved from being crumbling by her horrible cosmic dance.

This mother goddess is now mostly worshipped by the Hindu Bengalis, but she has devotees all over India and also in some foreign countries. In Malaysia she is known as Mariamma. Origin of this goddess may be traced back to the pre-Vedic age. The devout Hindus consider it as a grave sin to look at her nude image. So in most of the temples symbol or her bust is worshipped. In the great festival of the Bengalis known as Kali Puza her full image is adorned with a sari. Real tantrics, free from all vices, however, may worship her nude image.

She is both a benevolent and destructive goddess. Her worship is to be performed with proper devotion and perfect rituals. The priests are very careful to avoid minor irregularities which may invite her wrath. Honest and ethical devotees of this goddess are guarded against all evil forces outside and the vices inside. Tantric worship gives one magic power but these should never be misused or used to harm others or fulfill vile desires like lust. The fake tantrics who misuse the power acquired by tantric cult are punished by the goddess. In earlier times the robbers in Bengal used to worship her to acquire power for performing their mischief and ultimately they were punished by the goddess.'

After relating the account of the goddess Nil assured them that notwithstanding her apparently angry disposition, the goddess is basically an affectionate mother and forgives all mischief if atonement is made in the proper way and Nil would try his best to appease the goddess so that she forgave the hill people whatever be their fault in the past.

Nil went into bed late at night and dreamt that he was inside a dense forest at the feet of goddess Kali adorned with a red sari and golden ornaments scintillating with jewels. He prayed to her to forgive the innocent hill people whose ancestors might have committed some sin of which they were unaware. The goddess smiled affectionately and assured Nil that she would heed to his prayer but only after he had gone through the difficult tastes she would put him to. She would test his honesty, character, perseverance, patience, tolerance and dedication. He would be subjected to hazards and temptations which he would

have to overcome. The goddess said that the Lepcha girl was a divine entity but she was completely unaware of it. She had strong fascinations for Nil but Nil should be careful not to indulge in any physical relation with her.

He woke late and assured the Lama that he was now confident that he would be able to appease the goddess and persuade her to forgive the hill people. He took complete rest for the day and left for Siliguri the next day to meet his trekkers at New Jalpaiguri railway station. Doma bade him good bye and said in tearful eyes, 'I'll be looking for your return.'

Chapter 3: The Lady Professor

For the first few days after Nil's return to Calcutta, his head remained jammed with the novel situation he had been forced into by circumstances, the hill people, the Lama, the mysterious curse of goddess Kali and above all the Lepcha girl Doma. Her tearful morose countenance at the time of his departure came to the surface of his mind but he restrained his thought by remembering the exhortations of the goddess about the divinity of the girl in his last dream at the hills.

Soon his mind got diverted to his research works at the institute of the Bengali industrialist and exporter Mr. Rajib Mitra. The institute was situated at the third floor of a multi storied building called

'Mitra Mansion' at the junction of Camac Street and Park Street. The entry of Mr. Mitra in the educational business had been very recent. He at first started a management institute offering MBA courses and thereafter only a year ago started this research institute. This was an innovative idea of Mr. Mitra. The reception counter was at the ground floor of the building, and at the first and second floors management classes were held and the other floors above the third accommodated offices for his other businesses. Nil was working in this research institute ever since its inception one year ago. After completion of his Masters degree in economics he had at first joined as a lecturer at a degree college at Calcutta. He resigned as he could not accommodate himself with the nonacademic and unethical atmosphere there. Most of the teachers did not take classes and used to earn money by private coaching, the administration and governing body were under the influence of the ruling political party and were associated with various corrupt practices. Resigning from the college he took up the job of a freelance journalist and soon made a good name. He had no brothers and sisters and his father, a bank officer, was yet to retire from job. So he had no family obligations and the earning from journalism was enough to carry on his livelihood. In the meantime he completed his doctorate degree on industrial economics and his guide introduced him to Mr. Mitra who proposed Nil the idea of his research institute and Nil readily agreed and the institute started with Nil and later on many other research scholars joined it.

The researchers under the institute used to conduct surveys, individually or in groups over investment potential for foreign investors in various fields in India and reports were prepared on the basis of the surveys. These were sold in the international information market for foreign investment. Sometimes, the state governments or the Government of India bought these reports to decide upon the areas of foreign investment.

Nil had already collected, before his hill trekking, materials based on investment potential in the

arena of mining in the districts of Bankura of West Bengal. He had made exhaustive surveys in this regard and consulted libraries on rules, regulations and official procedures in India for the investors. Now he had to arrange these materials in an orderly fashion and prepare the final report.

Nil soon got absorbed in this arduous task and everything pertaining to the hill people and his accidental involvement with their problem was relegated to the back chamber of his memory. After preparing the initial draft of the article, he informed the institute that he would submit his complete report by a week or thereabouts. Now he had to do some computer work and so he went to the institute and directed the computer operator to insert the data, he had collected and written neatly on sheets of paper, in the statistical software. He told that he would come again the next day to complete the processing job (tables, charts, statistical analysis etc.) from the inserted data.

He never liked to use the lift, especially, while going downstairs. So he started climbing down the stairs being absorbed in the plan of the article and he took a start as soon as he approached the second floor as he heard a female voice calling him, 'hello Mr. Roy, you're here!'

Nil looked up and was astonished to find Mrs. Rita Sen walking towards him. As she came close by Nil replied promptly, 'I work here in a research project and has come today to process some data for my next research article. But I too ask you how you happened to be here.'

'Oh you don't know, I had resigned the college job a few months after your resignation and joined this management institute.'

'Which subject do you teach here?'

'Business Logistics.'

'But I think it was not in B. Com. Courses at college.'

'You're right. But I also taught at IGNOU (Indira Gandhi Open University) center of the college and I was requested to teach this new subject at M.Com. Courses as nobody else was willing to teach the subject. In course of teaching the subject I have gathered much knowledge on it and I'm now capable of teaching this new subject at this institute.'

She paused for a while and then continued, 'as far as I know the research unit has been created only a year ago and I think you've joined it very recently.'

'No I've joined it from its very inception.'

Mrs. Sen squinted and said, 'surprise, you've been working here for one year and our paths did not cross!'

'In fact my works are mainly outdoor job and I come here only to submit my article or for computer work while data processing becomes necessary. But now our paths have crossed.' Nil laughed aloud and Rita joined him.

'That's my good luck. But we should better go to the canteen and talk over coffee, of course, if you can afford time', she proposed.

Nil laughed and said, 'oh sure. I've plenty of time to while away now.'

They walked leisurely downstairs to the canteen which was congested now with gossiping office staff and only a few seats at the far end were vacant. They moved on to the corner and took two chairs.

'Checkup the menu and select the item of your preference', Rita forwarded the menu to Nil.

'My stomach is full as I've already taken heavy food from a restaurant. So infusion without sugar would be enough for me. You may however take whatever you like and I won't mind.' Nil returned the menu to her.

She called the waiter and ordered one omelet and two cups of coffee and continued conversation. She would be now around thirty two, at least three years older than Nil, but in her tight fitted orange sari sporting the navel and the heavy bums bulging out of the slim waistline, the red low-cut blouse displaying the sharp cleavage below the neckline, eyelashes trimmed neatly, hair closely fitted into a chignon and with her shining eyes and sharp nose she looked barely twenty five. Nil had heard she had no children even after five years of marriage. She also was not going on well with her husband but it was beyond courtesy to show curiosity about her personal life. She initiated the conversation after coffee was served.

'Do you know I queried about you after you had resigned abruptly but nobody in the college could tell anything about your whereabouts and the reason for your resignation. I called you at your land phone and learnt from your mother that you had been abroad. Where had you been, USA?'

Nil laughed aloud and said, 'oh that's a lie. In fact I had been at Patna at first and thereafter here in this city and instructed my parents to mislead everyone calling me so that nobody could disturb me.'

'My god, what a crazy boy you are! Why did you resign so abruptly?'

'Because I didn't like the unethical milieu there.'

'You're really very serious and rigid about your principles and that's why I like you so much. A young man of your age used to wear such a grave countenance at college that you were nicknamed jethu (elder brother of father).'

She started giggling like a teenager and Nil could not help joining her laughter.

'Anyway, what did you do after your resignation before you joined this job here?'

'After resigning from the college I took up freelance journalism and still doing it. I also started my

Ph. D work and was awarded the degree just before I joined here.'

Rita almost leapt up in excitement and shook hands with Nil and said ecstatically, 'what a news, you're now Dr. Roy.'

'Better call me simply Nil. It is more pleasant to me.'

'You're a naughty boy and it would be pleasant to me if you too call me Rita instead of Mrs. Sen. I've forgotten to tell you that I got my divorce last year and I demanded no alimony. The separation was by mutual consent.'

Nil was not at all interested in her personal matters and to divert the topic he asked, 'do you get good students here?'

'Yes, most of them are brilliant and very serious. I'm to study much to meet their queries and also I've to prepare the study material that takes a lot of my time but I feel very satisfied. You must agree that at that college there was very little to teach as most of the students did not attend classes and relied more on private couching than lessons at college classes. We could have forgotten our subjects if stayed there for a longer time.'

'I fully agree with you and that's the main reason of my resignation', Nil said seriously.

'You now look very fresh but still grave like a jethu', Rita started giggling and gesticulating awkwardly, the end of her sari dropped to reveal distinctly the vast cleavage below the neckline. Nil looked aside to avoid embarrassment but joined her laughter saying, 'does my laughter substantiate your view about me?'

Still giggling she said, 'I was just teasing you.'

'Then you're a dangerous lady.'

'If you think so. Anyway, I have an important class now, and I'd miss your lively company. Here's my card and call me please at my mobile number given in the card and inform me when you come to this office the next time.'

She left in an ecstatic mood and Nil felt relieved that he had not told her that he would come here the next day. He moved on to the Park Street and lighted a cigarette from a footpath stall. He was really amazed at her coquetry and remembered that at college many colleagues used to joke about her fascination for him. Her behavior today could be explained in many ways. This could be simply as game or real fascination for him. Whatever it was, it must be a temptation and he would have to guard himself against such temptations. He remembered the caution of the goddess in the dream and thought he would have to avoid meeting her the next day.

He tossed her card into the dust bin and moved to the railings at the corner of the footpath and started watching the vast moving line of vehicles along the Park Street. He took a start and turned his head by instinct as a hand fell on his shoulder from behind and he was elated beyond measure to find his college friend Shyamal Banerjee standing with a smiling face right behind him. Both of them got ecstatic and hugged each other warmly.

Shyamal was looking intently at the face of Nil which embarrassed Nil and he asked 'why do you look at me like that?'

Shyamal burst into laughter and said, 'you're now grown up my friend. You were so shy about girls at college and always felt nervous before them and now you were so much engrossed in gossip with a hot lady.'

'What do you mean?'

'I'd been in the canteen and you failed to notice me and me too did not like to disturb you. How did you hook up this voluptuous lady?'

'You are utterly mistaken my friend. There's nothing between us. She used to work with me in the same college from where I resigned about five years back and I came upon her after a long time.'

'Sorry, but her looks indicated that she has deep fascination for you. What a luck! I'm also acquainted with this lady and she always wears a grave look. For the first time I noticed her in jovial mood. So, my friend go ahead and my congratulations for you.'

Nil slapped Shyamal on the back and said, 'do you know she is much older than me?'

'So what? She still looks like a young girl and frighteningly hot and horny and above all she's a divorcee and loves you.'

'Go on saying whatever you like. I cannot restrain your tongue. But I think you have much fascination for her. Why don't you have a try?'

'Do you think I've not but all in vain. She would never be informal with me and now I understand the reason. She was waiting for her lost love and now she has got you. Hang on my lucky friend.'

'Let her and her love go to hell, I've other things to do than being the plaything of a spoilt lady.'

'My friend, don't be so harsh with her. I bet she loves you and she's not a spoilt lady. I've never seen her flirting with anybody.'

'You better live with your imagination and let us talk some different topic. What are you doing now?'

'I'm the chief of the sales department of a Punjabi firm dealing in agricultural commodities.'

'At college you had the ambition of being an IPS (Indian Police Service) officer.'

'I changed my ideas later on to discover the abject condition of the high ranking police officers in India. They are simply the servants of the ruling political parties. Now there's very little bossism here in my firm and I find the sales job a challenging and innovative one. Tell me now about your college job and how you happened to be here with this research department of Mr. Mitra.'

Nil informed Shyamal at length about his college job, his resignation, journalist's profession, securing doctorate degree and the connection that had brought him to this firm.

They moved into a restaurant and talked on their nostalgic college life. They exchanged their mobile numbers and parted company with the assurance that they would keep in touch. Before departure Shyamal again reminded him to maintain the relation with Rita and Nil angrily remarked, 'don't utter her name before me anymore.'

Shyamal set his car on gear and remarked after starting the car, 'okay my friend I would no longer poke my nose into your personal matters if you don't like.'

Nil started walking along the footpath to get to the metro railway station and he felt that Shyamal was right that Rita had deep fascination for him. Many incidents at college came alive from his memory. But he should be careful now. He too was feeling some attraction for her and he would have to overcome this temptation. This might be the first difficult test of the goddess. Suddenly his mind drifted on to Doma and further back to Mili and her invitation to bed. He had at first given way to temptation but could eventually dissociate himself from Mili. He was now confident to overcome temptation from both Rita and Doma. It would not be difficult to avoid Rita but Doma who would accompany him in the mission might be a difficult hurdle. Nil prayed to goddess Kali for strength of mind to overcome all temptations from the females.

Returning to his house he called Mr. Mitra and requested him not to disclose his address and contact numbers to anybody else as a safeguard against commercial espionage by other firms. But the real reason was to avoid contact with Rita. He along with his parents had recently shifted from their rented house at Dum Dum to a house bought at Barahnagar. None except Mr. Mitra and the sub-editor of a daily were informed of this change of address.

He went to bed early and fell fast asleep. His sleep broke at midnight and he felt amazed to think of the series of unexpected incidents in quick succession – the hill people and his intended mission to rescue them, the hill girl Doma and sudden encounter with Rita and Shyamal. He fell asleep again and dreamt of Rita kissing him madly that incited his passion and led to eventual rhythmic union and in course of the upheaval her face got transformed into Doma's and then again to Mili's. Then the scene changed all of a sudden and he discovered himself falling down a fathomless dark pit and his sleep broke. He was embarrassed to the moist sensation between his legs. The falling in the dark pit too had significance – in his dream he had surrendered to temptation that led to his fall into darkness. The erotic dream was for sure his repressed longings, Nil thought and was very much perturbed.

Next day he went to the office in the afternoon and went upstairs by the lift and asked the computer operator to upload the data in his pen drive so that he might do the processing job at his own computer. He got down by the lift and left the office immediately. He took a bus for central Calcutta and there in a Kali temple he prayed for a long time for power to overcome the temptations.

Chapter 4: The Journalist

For the next few days Nil remained engrossed in the report and completing the report he sent it by e- mail to the office of Mitra. As soon as he was relieved of the heavy burden of work a feeling of utter

blankness took possession of his heart. He could not decide upon the work he was to get engaged in to be relieved of the emptiness. Soon the memories of the hill returned and the sweet face of Doma came to the surface of his mind and an uncanny ecstatic feeling coursed through him. He spontaneously started humming a modern Bengali song, but it was interrupted as his mobile phone rang. The call was from the office of 'Smart News', a daily he used to write articles in. He heard the voice of a sub-editor and thought it would be a request for some new article.

But he was thrilled to learn that Sangey Tamang, their staff reporter at Gangtok, had come to Calcutta to have some personal talks with Nil. If Nil agreed he may give him Nil's mobile number. Nil asked if he was in the office and the sub-editor said he might be in the toilet. Nil told him to give Mr. Tamang his number and request him to call Nil as early as possible. He guessed it was something to do with the hill staff and his mind got a thrilling sensation. After a while the desired call came. He was right. Sangey was sent by the Lama to contact Nil.

'The matter cannot be discussed over phone and tell me whenever you're free to have face to face talk and where to meet you', Sangey said in a hushed tone.

'I'm free all through the day. You may meet me at my house anytime today before evening. If you're free you may come to my house right now', Nil replied.

'That would be fine but how to get to your house?'

'You take any bus or minibus that goes via Sinthee junction and get down at the junction. Call me after the bus crosses Shyambazar and I'll be waiting for you at the bus stop.'

'Okay, I'll start after lunch and likely to reach Sinthee by about 2 p.m. I've gone to Barrackpore several times by bus and so it would be no problem for me.'

Nil finished his lunch in time and after a few minutes' rest proceeded for the Sinthee more and the call came at about 1.35 p.m. and Sangey got down from bus just a few minutes before two. Nil could easily recognize him by his features and after they had exchanged greetings Nil took him right into his drawing room.

Sangey took a glass of water and seated comfortably on the sofa came to business,

'I'm well acquainted with the Lama at the Lepcha village and the family of the blessed girl. In fact, my father in law, a distant relative of Yalmo Lepcha, still resides in the village. I learnt the detail of the curse from my father in law but could never guess that I could be of any help to them in this matter. So I was a bit puzzled when my wife informed me that Doma, her childhood friend, had come to our house

and asked her to send me right to the Lama's cottage as soon as I returned from Gangtok at the weekend. I hurried to the cottage of the Lama who took me to confidence and gave me a brief idea about your sacred mission. He requested me to meet you and inform you that everything is ready and they are waiting for your arrival to initiate the mission. I at once agreed to the proposal and I knew that I could easily get your contact number from our paper's office at Calcutta. Tell me now when it would be possible for you to

visit the village. Remember that the mission may take a few months and you should decide your travel plan accordingly. You may take some time to decide and inform me later on over cell phone.' Sangey looked at Nil with questioning eyes.

'No need of much thinking. I've completed the project at hand and not likely to undertake any new project right now. So it would be no problem for me to spend a few months in the hills now.' Nil said with assurance.

'What about your office?'

'I've much freedom and perfect understanding with Mr. Mitra and therefore, there would be no problem from his side. I'll propose a visit to North Bengal for a few months to conduct a survey of the Terai region and investment opportunities there and he would for sure gladly accept the proposal.'

Sangey handed out a file from his bag and said, 'I was also asked by the Lama to collect some background information about you – your strong points and weaknesses – so that they could take precautions and appropriate measures accordingly. Here's the report and you please go through them and suggest if any modification is necessary.'

'How have you collected the information about my past?' Nil asked.

Sangey said, 'I went first to Mitra Mansion, the address you had left with the Lama. I thought I'd get both your background and present address from your office. I happened to meet one Mrs. Sen there who helped me a lot about your background. But she told she was unaware about your present address and contact number. Only the proprietor Mr. Mitra may know this and I could not contact him as he was outstation. Then an idea occurred to me that you are a freelance journalist and my office may help me about your whereabouts and I was right. Now the report of your background at your first job at college is written in the following pages. I've got all these information from Mrs. Sen who told she had been your colleague at the college. You go through them and tell me if she has given correct information.'

Nil felt a bit perturbed at the mention of Mrs. Sen. But he took care not to reveal his feelings in his face and to this end he overplayed himself and said enthusiastically, 'O.K. leave the report with me. I'll go through it tonight and make modifications if necessary. Now tell me your next plan.'

Sangey said, 'I've some works here. It would take a week at the most and thereafter I'd leave by plane. It would not be safe for you to go by flight that may attract attention of unwanted persons. So you try to book ticket by Darjeeling Mail as early as possible.'

Nil called his travel agent who informed that tickets of Darjeeling Mail would not be available for the next sixty days. He could, however, travel anytime by the Tista Torsha Express but the journey would be troublesome and lengthy. Then checking up again the travel agent said that only a few tickets were available for 26th of that month. But it was an inauspicious day for the Hindus. Nil said that he had no superstitions and requested the agent to book a ticket for that day.

At night he opened the file and went through it and was amazed to find the vivid and exact information given by Rita. She had remembered all these for such a long time. Nil himself could not have given such details. He got a start to think of Rita's keen interest in him. Was it true love? Anyway, whatever it was he ought not to fall in the trap and spoil his noble mission.

Next day he decided to disclose everything about the mission to Shyamal as he was a reliable person. He contacted Shyamal over mobile phone and met him at his residence at Rasbehari Avenue. Shyamal listened to him with rapt attention and after Nil had detailed him about the mission, Shyamal looked very much impressed and said,

'I encourage you whole heartedly about the sacred mission. By the way, what is your own opinion about the tantric? Do you think he's a real benefactor of the hill people?'

'The hill people including the Lama believes so but to me the tantric appears to be a complicated person.'

'I may help you to some extent in this regard. You told me the tantric had been to Tarapith before he settled in the hills.'

'Exactly.'

'My wife's guru is a renowned tantric who had resided at Tarapith for a long time. So he might know the tantric in the hills.'

'Thanks for the information, but where does the guru reside now and how can I meet him?'

'Now he is staying near Nimtala burning ghat but nobody can meet him without prior appointment. Anyway I'll arrange for an appointment through my wife and inform you over cell phone accordingly.'

'But make it as early as possible. I'll leave for North Bengal on twenty sixth.'

'I'm going to his ashram right now and arranging for the meeting. Nil-da rest assured it won't be later than twenty third', Sima, Shyamal's wife, assured.

At night Sima called Nil and said, 'gurudev has consented to meet us the day after tomorrow after 8 p.m. when he is free from the visitors.'

'Should I go to your house or go direct to Nimtala?' Nil asked.

'Why should you take trouble to come over here. We'll be waiting for you outside the Bhutnath temple at Nimtala after 7 p.m.'

Sima handed over the receiver to Shyamal and the two friends talked for some time.

In the evening Shyamal and Sima were waiting in front of the temple when nil arrived at Nimtala. They waited for some time and after the last visitor had left the tantric guru came out of the temple and

they offered him pramam. He directed them to follow him. The tantric in red robe was tall and had a broad shoulder and curled hair. He had a large red mark on his forehead, sharp nose and brilliant eyes. There were several garlands of rudrakshas in his neck. His residence was close to the Anandamoyee kali temple and it was a one storey wooden house with a drawing room for visitors, a bed room and a small kitchen. A timber merchant and devotee had gifted the guru the house. Nil, Shyamal and Sima waited while the tantric guru entered his bed room for rest. After some rest the guru came out and laying in reclining position on the armchair queried Nil about the hill matters. Nil related everything since his mishap in the snow storm. The guru listened to him with rapt attention. After Nil had finished, the guru said in a grave tone, 'it's unquestionably a risky mission but still I advise you to go ahead.' He then passed on to the tantric in the hills.

'I know him very well. He was my disciple to start with. He is indeed a very powerful and dedicated tantric but thirst for power might have spoilt him. I advised him to be free from power mongering in order to make further spiritual advancement. But he was aggrieved at my advice and left me and fell in the trap of a crazy Kapalic and left with him. Thereafter I knew nothing about his whereabouts. Now I learnt from Mina that he is in the hills and I'm afraid he is engaged in mischief. Nothing is impossible for a

misguided tantric. But we cannot come to any conclusion about that without definite evidence. His exhortations of helping the hill people may be true. After all he is a good person and he could have been a great spiritual man but for his morbid love for power. All is Ma Kali's lila.'

The guru asked nil to get closer and inspected his forehead and displayed a broad smile and said, 'it's time for meditation and I'll have to leave.' Then turned toward Nil and said, 'go ahead with the mission and unravel the mystery in the hills.'

They came out of the guru's residence and on his way back Nil thought that the smile of the guru after examining his forehead indicated that the trident mark might be really significant as believed by the hill people.

The journey was finalized at last and Nil informed Sangey the detail of his journey and the approximate time of his arrival at Manebhanjan from where the journalist would pick him up.

Chapter 5: The Mysterious Bhutia

Nil decided that he would go direct to Darjeeling from New Jalpaiguri (NJP) and visit the beautiful hill town for three days and thereafter go right to Manebhanjan on the appointed date. The train was an hour late. A co-passenger suggested him to go by auto to Tensing Norgay bus terminus and he would get plenty of buses and land rovers from there. Vehicles from NJP would charge exorbitant rates. Nil deposited his luggage at the cloak room at the station and got refreshed from the first class waiting room. He then went to the railway canteen for breakfast. He suddenly felt uneasy to notice a gigantic Bhutia in shabby clothes glancing at him curiously from a seat at the far end of the canteen. He had a large head and

wide forehead; longish hair tied at the back and as he grinned his ugly yellowish teeth gave the impression of a demon. It was not cold at all at the station but the Bhutia was wearing a grey shabby coat that ran down to his knees and as he stood up Nil observed that he was very tall and stout and notwithstanding his uneasiness Nil could not but laugh at the awkward appearance of the man. He had heard that these

Bhutias do not bathe and they never put off the garments until they are torn. He had also heard that the stench from their body is horrible. There might be exaggerations, but all these made him laugh within and free from the worries that the looks of the giant had generated within him. Generally these people are simple and harmless and he might have looked at Nil out of seer curiosity and he looked malicious simply because of his natural appearance. Soon Nil forgot the man. At the bus terminus the next bus was to start after one hour. A Nepali boy approached him that there was a seat at a land rover and he might go by it to save time. Nil had earlier bitter experience of journey by packed up land rovers. He had no hurry and he decided to take the bus. From tourist counter he booked a room for three days at a hotel at Darjeeling.

The bus journey was pleasant and the beautiful sceneries on the way enchanted him. The hotel was near the railway station and he had no difficulty in finding it. The porter who carried his luggage took him right to the hotel.

He visited the town for three days and on the fixed date he took the bus for Shukia Pokri as suggested by the hotel manager. Vehicles for Manebhanjan were available from this place. Nil bargained with a small car, the cheapest vehicle and at last they came upon an agreed rate. He went to a nearby stall and bought chewing gums and a bottle of water that would be necessary on the way. While approaching the

car he was panicked to find the same Bhutia talking with the driver of the car. As Nil got closer the man greeted him and there was no stench from his body and now he was wearing a different coat and his hairstyle was a bit different, but from his looks Nil had no doubt that he was the same man. As Nil got into the car, the man asked Nil if he was in need of hotels at Manebhanjan. If so he might give Nil the address of his own hotel which was very good but cheap too. Nil replied that he had already booked hotel

there. The man greeted revealing his yellow stained teeth and left. Nil thought he could surely be the same man and following him. 'But who has appointed him and why?', the question started pinching him. Then he tried his best to drive away the idea thinking that they were two different persons and simply from his inward worries he was suspecting him to be a spy.

Sangey was waiting for him at Manebhanjan. He said, 'let's have tea first and then proceed for

Rimbik. After a night's halt there at a hotel we'll proceed for the village.'

They took tea and singara from a stall and Nil once again noticed the Bhutia in a different outfit, standing at a corner and watching them. As Nil glanced at him he promptly hid himself behind a vehicle. Nil got out of the shop and searched for him but he was nowhere to be found. On their way to Rimbik in the car hired by Sangey, Nil related the incident to Sangey who laughed and said, 'Mr. Roy, you're not accustomed to seeing Bhutias and therefore all Bhutias look alike to you. There are plenty of them in the hills and I'm sure these three Bhutias you've seen are different persons. So give up your unnecessary worries.'

Sangey might be right Nil thought, but still the anxiety went on lingering in his mind.

Was the Bhutia spying on him, but why? What could be his purpose and who could have appointed him? Nil did not find any answer and disquiet of his mind continued like the irritation caused by a tiny thorn insight the flesh. It could as well be all figments of his imagination due to repressed tension. He tried to convince himself that Sangey was right that all these three persons were different and as he was unaccustomed to seeing the Bhutias, they appeared alike to him. Still he could not shake off his worries which remained hidden in the depth of his mind and caused a continued disquiet. To divert his mind Nil started conversation with Sangey.

'Shall we go via Sandhak-fu?' Nil queried.

'No this time we would take a different route', Sangey smiled and continued, 'from Rimbik we'll go by a vehicle to Gorkay valley and thereafter on foot to the village. This would be safe as we are likely to meet very few people on the way.'

'Would it take a very long time to reach the village along this route?'

'No, it is like to take a shorter time but the route is a bit difficult. We are to climb steep rises and cross a few gorges over rope bridges.'

Nil felt a bit perturbed to learn about the rope bridges. He said, 'I've never crossed rope bridges'.

'I'll give you direction and with a little effort you'll be able to cross them. It would be an adventure trekking with new experience and the natural view on the way is fantastic.'

Assurance of Sangey was not enough to allay Nil's worries about the rope bridges but it had one good effect on him. He completely forgot the Bhutia.

It was afternoon when they arrived at Rimbik and they went right to the hotel already booked by Sangey. The weather was now colder and Nil had to wear a sweater. After dinner Nil went out to by cigarettes from a stall to the other side of the road across from the hotel. While lighting the cigarette he turned around and his heart pounded to notice the Bhutia only a few feet from the shop. He was now wearing a heavy woolen sweater and stepped into the darkness to find Nil turning his glance at him. Nil

had now no doubt it was the same person. At Shukia Pokri he could watch the Bhutia from close and he now found the same scar on his right cheek. Nil hastened to the hotel and did his best to tame the trepidations of his heart. It was no use telling the matter to Sangey as he would again give the same explanation and would have doubt about the divine power of Nil.

In bed Nil could not sleep for a long time. No doubt the Bhutia was spying on him and someone must have appointed him. But who could be behind him? The only person, who might be interested to know the whereabouts of Nil, was the tantric at the cursed plateau, but how did he learn about the mission? Neither Sangey nor Shyamal could be suspected. The, tantric at Nimtala, however, might have some contact with his erstwhile disciple in the hills. He was a new acquaintance of Shyamal. He had come to Nimtala from Tarapith and erected a temple of goddess Kali near the burning ghat and soon the temple and the man became very popular. People believed that he could resolve all sorts of problems. Shyamal's son had

some speech problem and renowned doctors had suggested that he would not be able to talk till the age of six. Then with the advice of a friend at Ahiritola, Mina had visited the tantric who soon cured the child and his speech became normal at the age of three only one month after he had been blessed by the tantric. Thereafter Mina became his disciple and since then both Shyamal and Mina had deep faith in him. But besides his curing power they knew nothing else about him.

Nil now suspected that the tantric guru had misled him. The guru was still in close contact with his erstwhile disciple and informed him about Nil's mission. What the guru told about the power mongering of his disciple might also be true for him. It was not unlikely that through his disciple he was trying to create a strong following among the hill people. If his disciple was successful in resolving their problem, even if after some years, this would spread the fame of both him and his guru. If so the tantrics would never like a third person winning the hill people from them. So he should be very cautious about the Bhutia spy.

Nil did not discuss the spy issue any more with Sangey, but he remained alert all along. Before

getting into the vehicle for Gorkay he checked up all the places around and was satisfied as no trace of the Bhutia could be found. The track to Gorkay was steep and through forest and on the way he found only a few Nepalese collecting fuel wood. The valley was beautiful and had much resemblance with the Lepcha village. It too looked like a cauldron surrounded by hills covered with tall pines but unlike the barren Lepcha village the place was lush with green vegetables. A beautiful rivulet was flowing through the village and there were a few shops and tea stalls. They rested at a trekkers' hut and took lunch prepared

on order by a Nepali family. All the villagers were Nepalese and among them any Bhutia could be easily distinguished. Nil bought cigarettes from a stall and asked the shopkeeper if other hill races used to frequent the village. The shopkeeper replied that at times Lepcha and Limbu people visited the village to buy vegetables but no Bhutia had ever visited the village. This gave Nil satisfaction that if the Bhutia attempted to follow him here too he could be detected as his presence would raise curiosity among the villagers and he would not be safe in an unknown village.

After they had left Gorkay, the gentle uphill journey was pleasant at first but soon it turned difficult. They had to climb steep slopes along a narrow causeway skirting the sides of a hill and any false step meant a fall into the deep gorge. Moreover he had to be very cautious as the narrow path was strewn with pine needles. Still the journey was thrilling and adventurous. Then came the most difficult part – crossing a deep valley along a rope bridge. Ropes were attached with trees on both sides of the valley. The valley would have to be crossed by keeping legs on one rope and holding a rope above. Sangey crossed the bridge several times to make Nil confident. And eventually Nil could make it uttering silently the name of goddess Kali. Sangey carried the entire luggage over the bridge. Now the journey was downhill and less difficult but the chance of skidding on pine needles increased and Nil had to move very cautiously. They had to cross two more rope bridges and Nil had already learnt to cross them effortlessly.

It was almost afternoon when they arrived at a shallow valley in between two adjacent hillocks. Sangey told that it would not be judicious to go direct to the village and so they took the causeway to the Lama's cottage.

Nil was received cordially by the Lama, Yalmo and Doma. The boy ran toward them and snatched the luggage from their hands. He looked very happy to meet Nil after a long time. Nil queried Doma

about her mother, brother and sisters. For sake of secrecy his arrival was kept from her brother and sisters. It was evening and Sangey had to stay the night at the cottage.

Nil did not disclose anything about the Bhutia to Doma or the Lama. But he was curious to know if any Bhutia resided in this locality. He asked Doma, 'does any Bhutia live around this place? I'm very much curious about these simple Buddhists.'

Doma replied, 'none lives close to our village but there's a Bhutia village far downhill to the northern side of the cursed plateau. They are really very simple people and devotees of Lord Buddha. But I've learnt that some of them have now become devotees of goddess Kali and occasionally visit the tantric's temple to offer prayer to the goddess.'

The information made it more probable to Nil that the Bhutia was a spy of the tantric who might be already informed of Nil's association with the Lepchas, even about the mission. Two possibilities crossed his mind. First the tantric needed the assistance of Lepcha laborers for some esoteric practice to achieve higher spiritual power. In such a case he would not resolve the curse fully until completion of his esoteric practice. Secondly it was also probable that by resolving the curse the tantric was expecting to spread his influence over the Lepchas and his guru at Calcutta might also be involved in it. In either case he would not like meddling by Nil in the matter and would try his best to foil Nil's mission the success of which would spoil his goal.

Nil remembered the dream where the goddess had cautioned him that in his mission he would have to encounter hazards both from outside and from within. The tantric and the spy were outside hazards, but he would have also to be cautious about the hazards from within. The temptation from Rita was no longer consequential as she was now far off. But Doma, who was deeply infatuated in him, might be a problem

as he too had a subconscious desire for her. He would have to apply all his mental strength to overcome this weakness.

After early dinner they went to the secret room to discuss the plan in detail. Sangey was not needed for the purpose and he went to bed in the front room. The Lama now gave the detail of the mission chalked out jointly by him and the Hindu Sage at Nepal.

At first Nil and Doma would visit the cursed place secretly. Nil with his trident mark and Doma with her divine power would be free from the evil effects of the curse. The tantric should by no means know about their visit. This would aggrieve him and he would stop whatever help he was providing to them. They still needed his help until the curse could be fully removed by Nil and Doma. So they should visit the place secretly. Every night the tantric remained absorbed in deep meditation but by his supernatural power he would be able to know the presence of Nil and Doma at the plateau. To prevent this the Hindu sage had prepared a robe which would conceal them from the detecting power of the tantric. They could, however, be detected by the tantric's men if they visited the place along the common track. So they should now go to the Buddhist cave at the end of a Sherpa village. The Lama there had already been informed about the mission and he had assured that he would cooperate by all means. They would go there under the guise of performers of occult meditation of Lord Buddha and stay in hiding in the caves.

As Nil expressed curiosity about the caves, the Lama told that at the end of the Sherpa village to the north east of the cursed plateau there ware a few caves with antique Buddha statues curved on the stone walls. No body knew the history of the caves and to all the Buddhists the caves were very sacred. Sometimes Buddhist monks from distant places, even Tibet visited the caves and stayed there for secret religious practices. So it would not be difficult for the Lama there to convince any curious Sherpa that Nil and Doma were monk and nun from Sikkim practicing occult worship in the caves. With the robes on, they would look like Buddhist monk and nun and nobody would be able to recognize them.

Now staying in the caves they, with the assistance of the Lama there, would secretly visit the plateau at night and discover the nature of the curse. Their supernatural power would help them in this matter. They should first discover the center of the curse and thereafter take further decision accordingly, if necessary, consulting again the sage at Nepal.

They got up early next morning and after early breakfast prepared for the adventure. The robes reached up to their feet and covered their faces like burkhas. Now Nil looked like a high level Buddhist monk and Doma like a Buddhist nun. At the north east corner of the secret room there was a lowly door so long hidden behind a shelf. The Lama removed the shelf and opened the door which led them into a narrow cave and they had to crawl along the entire length of the cave to come out into the open. Doma giggled while brushing off the dusts from the robe of Nil and he felt a sensation of thrill while brushing off dust from Doma's robe. They were now inside a cluster of dwarf rhododendrons. The downhill path snaking through the gaps of the trees was very steep at places but Nil had no problem in climbing down by catching hold of the branches of the trees.

The atmosphere now was foggy and soon they were engulfed in dense fog. Nothing could be visible beyond a few feet. Doma got close to Nil and took hold of his hand so that Nil did not lose the way. She interlocked her arm with Nil's and the latter had to struggle hard to repress his emotions and nervousness. He now felt as though he was floating in the clouds hand in hand with an uncanny goddess. They stopped at places for a few minutes' rest when Nil felt tired. It was eleven o'clock when the fog started dissipating and the dim sun was visible through the translucent clouds. Nil looked around and observed that they had taken a semi-circular turn around the hill containing the cursed plateau and leaving the village behind. They had come far down and only the forest covered sides of the cursed plateau were now visible. The rhododendron forest had now become thinner and Nil realized they had gone down even below the level

of the village. They found a level ground in between the trees and sat down to have their lunch. Ahead of them a deep canyon had separated the hill from another hill and Nil could hear the murmurs of water inside the canyon. Doma told that the rivulet along the canyon had flowed into south Sikkim. Both this one and one that used to irrigate their village had their origins in a natural lake high up in the north east at the foot of the Kanchenjunga. This one, being free from curse, was flowing across Sikkim into the Tista River.

Nil asked if they would have to cross the canyon now. Doma replied that it could not be crossed here. They would have to follow an uphill path alongside the canyon and they would cross the river farther to the north east over the roof of a tunnel through which the river had flown. As they came close to the canyon, the river far below looked greenish and the scenic view made Nil spellbound.

After an hour's journey they came close to the roof of the tunnel. The scenery was fantastic and Nil stood transfixed watching the river coming out of the mouth of the tunnel and eddying around boulders strewn all along the gentle slope of the canyon to the right. Doma looked back and laughed to find Nil standing like a statue. She grabbed his hand and led him over to the mossy roof of the tunnel. The thick layer of mosses was spongy and squeaked at the pressure of their feet. The roof was about thirty feet long and fifteen feet wide. The shorter side had a gentle slope keeping with the slope of the canyon. From both sides of the roof that was a natural bridge, the river was flowing twenty feet below. The upper side of the roof down to the river was covered with creepers and mosses. On the lower side there was a steep causeway leading to the water.

Doma beckoned Nil to follow her and started climbing down the causeway and Nil followed her. Boulders were scattered all along the course of the river. They got close to the river and sat on a flat boulder. Doma put her hand into the water and started sprinkling water on all sides and giggled while Nil protested. Nil tried to retaliate but icy coldness of the water prevented him. This place of the canyon was wide and the river had flown through the boulders making multiple twists and turns and at places between boulders the water was stagnant and Nil was amazed to notice small fishes roaming around merrily.

Now Doma started humming a song in her dialect which appeared to Nil very sweet and romantic and the tune and rhythm of the song got mingled with the murmurs of the flowing water and Nil felt hilarious as though he was floating in air in an uncanny land. The sky had now become cloudy and Doma hastened up and said,

'hurry up, it will rain soon and we are to find a cover.'

'But what about your huge umbrellas?'

'They won't work. Rain here is generally accompanied by strong wind that breaks off or sweeps away umbrellas.'

She looked at the watch in Nil's wrist and exclaimed, 'my god it's already one o'clock. It would take at least three more hours from here to reach the caves and the last part of the journey is a very difficult one.'

Soon it started drizzling with gusts of wind and they had to open the umbrellas. But the eddying gusts made it very difficult to hold on to the umbrellas. By good luck they found a cave like opening by the side of the hill and it was at the leeward side of the wind. They got into the opening and soon the drizzle

turned into heavy downpour and the wind roared and raged across the hills. The rain, however, did not continue for more than half an hour and bright sun peeped through the stray clouds at the south west. They resumed their journey and came to a square level field covered with thick layer of grass. They would have to climb down the steep slope at the far end of the field and because of tiny springs rejuvenated by rain, it could be a very difficult climb down, Doma cautioned Nil.

They crossed the grassy field and came close to the mouth of the downhill track which had zigzagged down like the letter Z and suddenly a chill coursed down the spine of Nil as he noticed the Bhutia

standing behind a tree right at the opening of the downhill track. Nil drew down the covering of his face keeping only the eyes uncovered. The Bhutia came out of his hiding, bowed his head and getting close to Doma bowed again bending forward his tall body and asked in Nepali (the common language for hill people speaking different dialects), 'mother, you two must be sacred Buddhist pilgrims I suppose.'

Doma replied, 'you're right. We're from north Sikkim, going to visit the sacred caves. Is this the right way?'

The Bhutia replied, 'yes. About half a kilometer from here the path is divided into two. The left branch goes to our Bhutia village and the right one to the caves. But the steep downhill track straight to the caves is very risky. You may better take the easier track across the Sherpa village. Further down the track is bifurcated again and you can easily recognize the easier track from it's gentle slope.'

The Bhutia continued, 'my name's Namsell Bhutia. Don't forget to pray for me to the Lord in the caves. Best wishes for you.' He bowed again and moved to the other side of the field.

Nil looked nervous and asked Doma about the intention of the Bhutia. Doma assured him that he was a simple Bhutia. The red vermilion mark on his forehead indicated that he was a devotee of goddess Kali and probably he was now going to visit the tantric's temple.

Nil apprehended that Namsell was no doubt a spy of the tantric, had recognized them in spite of their robes and he was likely to follow them further up to the caves. Anyway he would have to encounter the hazards bravely and with a cool head and it would not be judicious to make Doma worried by disclosing the matter to her.

'Is the Bhutia village close by?' Nil asked.

Doma replied, 'it's about seven kilo meters downhill from here. After some distance this path is bifurcated. The one to the left leads to the Bhutia village and we're to follow the right one.'

The forest gradually became thinner and the path now was wider and pebbles were scattered on the path. They had to step very carefully to avoid being skidded by stepping on stray pebbles. They soon reached the bifurcation and took the rightward track.. About hundred feet further down the track was divided again. The rightward branch with a gentle slope had skirted the hill ahead and gone across the Sherpa village to the caves. They wanted to avoid the Sherpas and therefore started climbing down the steep causeway that led direct to the caves. From the divide, the caves, through the steep path, were around five kilo meters. The sky soon got overcast with dense clouds and it became almost dark.

All of a sudden the sky was torn apiece by lightning and the rumbling of the thunder shook the hills as though in an earthquake and it started raining heavily. Because of the strong wind the umbrellas could not be opened. No shelter was visible close by. The robes were made with waterproof materials but water, getting through the openings at their throats, drenched them thoroughly inside and Nil started shivering in cold. They got close to the trunk of a large tree and tried to save themselves from the onslaught of the torrents of rain and eddies of chilly wind.

Suddenly a horrible blast shook the hills and the continuing deep rumbling made them aware of

heavy landslide at the top of the hill and rolling down of huge boulders toward them. Doma blurted out in a panicked voice, 'let's immediately run away from this place. Heavy boulders are rolling down the hills and soon this place would be swept off. To save our lives we should now go uphill along the path we'd come down.'

They started racing uphill and could barely escape the boulders and rains of stones demolishing whatever came their way. Nil got exhausted but Doma started dragging him up along even after he was unconscious and she could ultimately reach a small cave like opening at a safe distance from the devastation. It was now pitch dark and it was still raining but at a slower pace.

After some time Nil regained consciousness and was embarrassed to discover his head on the lap of

Doma. He hastened to get up and Doma asked, 'do you feel comfortable now?'

'To some extent and where are we?' Nil asked

Doma smiled and said, 'we are at a safe place.'

'How long had I been unconscious?'

'Not more than an hour.'

'What to do now?'

'In this darkness we have nothing to do but to wait for the sky to be clear and then in moon light we may again climb down and see if there could be any path to proceed along toward the caves.'

'But we are to go without food for a long time and I'm already hungry.'

'Don't worry I've enough bread and dry fruits in by rucksack '

Nil felt that his robe and inner garments had been removed from his body and his bare body was covered with a thin blanket.'

In the dim light of the candle Doma had lighted he was embarrassed to see Doma too in the same condition and while talking occasionally her blanket slipped and her bare heavy breasts were visible.

She said, 'the rain has let up now and the wind would soon dry up the drenched garments.'

Doma was not worried at all nor was she embarrassed. She took out bread, fruits and water and they completed their eating.

Fortunately it was a full moon night and soon the moon came out in the clear sky and made the ambience uncanny. The garments had already dried now and Doma collected them from the dry rocks that had walled the cave and coming closer to Nil she removed the blanket from Nil and stacked it into the rucksack after folding it neatly. Nil was now with only a short underwear and Doma with a panty. She

was not at all concerned about their topless nudity but Nil got nervous and felt his passion rising.

Doma now came closer and they stood facing each other at only a few feet apart. Their expectant eyes met and Doma lowered her eyes in embarrassment. Nil felt the tremor of his extremities. He looked up and watched the semi nude goddess standing with passionate demeanor within the reach of his hands. He watched with passion her strong and beautiful legs, the triangular bulge in her panty, the heavy butts protruding at the back, the slim waist line, the round navel on the flat belly, and the large heaving boobs. Her eyes were fixed at the throbbing bulge between his legs. She raised her eyes and the four passionate eyes met again. They stood motionless for a while and all of a sudden both of them uttered loudly, 'we are on a sacred mission and we are to preserve our sanctity,' and they hastened to get dressed up.

They now climbed downhill and horrified to find that the track to the caves was completely demolished leaving only a polished hillside. Doma decided that they would again climb uphill now and approach the caves across the Sherpa village. The way to the village was out of the landslide zone. They moved uphill in quest of the track to the village and after long searches realized that in the mystic moon light they had lost their way and did not know where they were going. Still they continued searches for some time and at last decided to wait till the daybreak. Nil was now completely exhausted and he fell flat on a clean rock at the bottom of a large tree. Doma told that she would look for some better place for

night shelter. She directed Nil to wait at the place until her return. She hurried off and disappeared behind the cluster of pines.

Nil lay on his back and watched the hide and seek game of the moon and the dollops of clouds. He dozed for some time and woke by a horrible dream that he was being swept away by the landslide. He looked at the watch and got worried. More than an hour had elapsed and Doma had not yet returned. Out of worry he got up and started moving along the path Doma had followed. Even after half an hour's walk he still could find no trace of Doma. He felt completely exhausted and decided to return to the previous place and wait.

He turned around and made for the stone slab and was soon horrified to realize that the moon light had misguided him again and it would not be possible for him to get back to the stone. On the contrary, he might get farther away from the place. The moon was again covered with cloud and it started drizzling.

He got closer to the hill and finding a curved spot at the bottom of the hill he stepped into to protect himself from the rain. But he quickly moved back to find a large black snake and saw the round red eyes watching him and in a moment he closed his eyes to find its menacing hood high up about three feet from the ground. In a blank mind Nil waited for his destiny. But instead of the strike and death he heard a thumping sound and opening his eyes he was bewildered to find the head of the snake crushed by a slab of stone and the body still wriggling in desperation. He then heard the angry voice of Doma, 'what the hell did you leave the place for? You were sure dead and the mission spoilt if my instinct did not guide me

here on time.'

Nil could not speak and looked at her helplessly like a truant child caught by its mother while committing mischief. His helpless demeanor swept away her anger and she burst out laughing, but Nil could not join her as the horror still haunted him.

Doma said with feigned anger, 'naughty boy, never be disobedient again.' She was now pacified and told him why she had been late. She had found a good cave for shelter at a place she was familiar with. Thereafter she had gone downhill to collect some sweet roots that would add flavor to the bread. All of a sudden her sixth sense guided her to the spot where Nil was in danger.

They now moved for the cave she had found. On the way Nil felt dizzy and bad headache. But he did not disclose this to Doma and went on walking with utmost will power. At last they reached the shelter and Nil dropped down on the ground in utter exhaustion. Touching his forehead Doma found that he had temperature. She spread a blanket to make his bed and covered his body with another one. She now left again to collect the roots and some herbs to palliate fever.

As soon as she had left Nil felt asleep and started moaning.

Now Doma made haste and returned by half an hour and was worried to find Nil moaning. She touched his forehead again and found the temperature higher now. She took out the herb, pasted it on her palm and woke him up. Nil at first could not realize where he was but slowly his memory returned. She asked, 'how do you feel now?'

'Not very well, I feel my head heavy and painful'

He got up and in a reclining position took the herb paste which tasted extremely bitter but in a few minutes he felt better. Doma asked him to rest his head on her lap and he did not hesitate. She started fingering his forehead deftly and he soon fell asleep and it was a sound sleep without moaning or dreams. Both the blankets were in use by Nil. So Doma had to lie down on the stone floor of the cave. She was too tired and fell asleep but her sleep broke soon. Nil was still sleeping peacefully and moon rays had fallen

on his innocent face. Looking at the watch in his hand she found it was past midnight.

She could not make out what to do now. She went out of the cave and started walking aimlessly. The sky was now clear and the moon light had made the night dreamy. She hoped to find out the way to the Sherpa village and carry Nil to the caves. She went ahead and tried to guess in which direction the approach of the road could be. Suddenly she heard some voices and she walked in the direction of the voices and turning corner found Namsell with a few other shorter Bhutias searching hither and thither for something. She ran toward them and they looked up to hear her foot steps. Namsell came forward and said in a worried voice, 'mother where is the monk?'

'He's okay, sleeping in a safe cave but he has high fever.' Namsell heaved a sigh of relief and said, 'oh, I was very much worried about you. I've already informed the Lama at the caves and he with his men would soon reach this place and take you along through a roundabout route which is still undamaged.'

'But how you happened to be here at this hour?'

'I heard the rumbling of heavy land slide and then it dawned on me that by this time you and the monk might have reached near the site of land slide and was deeply worried. So I called these villagers and proceeded right for the site. Coming here I was terrified to observe the vast damage done by the landslide. We frantically looked for you but could not find any trail. I then consoled myself that you must have reached the caves before the disaster. To be confirmed I took a difficult climb down a steep hillside

keeping my men engaged in searching and went right to the caves and was really worried to learn that you had not gone there. The Lama too was terribly worried. The Lama learnt from me the location of this

place and said that he with some Sherpas from the village would soon reach this spot and requested me to wait here until he arrives. Thereafter I returned here and was waiting for the Lama. Fortunately I now find you alive and safe by the grace of the Lord. But still I'm a bit worried about the sick monk. Better show me the cave where the monk is so that I may guide the Lama to the spot.'

'Are you a Buddhist or a Hindu' Doma asked casually on their way.

Namsell replied, 'I'm a Buddhist peasant. My Tibetan ancestors were tantrics and so I worship goddess Kali also and practice tantric cult following family tradition.'

'Have you now become a disciple of the Hindu tantric at the plateau?'

Namsell laughed and replied, 'I think you make this guess from my visits to his temple. I just wanted to meet this great tantric but his Nepali disciples dissuaded me on the ground that the great tantric does not meet any non-Hindu. I still occasionally visit the sacred temple.'

Namsell left after Doma had shown him their shelter and he returned soon with the Lama and the

Sherpas and bade good bye after offering good wishes for the nun and the monk.

Chapter 6: The Caves

In the Buddhist cave Nil remained almost unconscious for two more days. He had an attack of a virus fever which could be fatal. Hill people were generally immune of this virus, but outsiders might be easily afflicted and killed. Both the Lama and Doma got worried about Nil and prayed to god for his cure. The Lama immediately informed an herbal doctor at an adjacent village. The nonagenarian doctor could not come himself but on the basis of the symptom of Nil's illness he sent some herbs instructing to administer them by inhalation. The three herbs were to be administered in succession with an interval of half an hour and the circle repeated. On the third day Nil regained consciousness and his temperature was normal. The headache had also subsided completely. But he was too weak to move. He had to take rest for at least a week.

Doma detailed to him every incident since he had fallen unconscious. Nil got a start to learn about the meddling of the Bhutia. He did not suppress the Bhutia issue any longer and gave her the detail of how he had been followed ever since he had arrived at the New Jalpaiguri railway station.

Doma laughed aloud and expressed the same view as Sangey had done earlier, 'all Bhutias look alike to one who encounters them for the first time. Namsell had never gone out of this place. Moreover he is very simple and helpful too. In fact only because of his assistance we could come out of the impasse without much trouble. Rest assured the Bhutias you came across at different place are all different persons.' Nil did not argue with her. He was quite sure that Namsell had lied to Doma that he had never gone out of this place. Each Bhutia might look alike to his unaccustomed eyes but each was not likely to have the scar on his face. But it still remained a mystery why Namsell (the spy of the tantric for sure) had taken so much trouble to save them and help them reach the caves safely. After some thinking it was clear to Nil that Namsell must have done this by the instruction of the tantric who wanted to learn about their mission and did not desire their death at this stage. If they were allowed to proceed further with the

mission the tantric would be able to spoil it at the last stage and prevent any future efforts on the part of the Lepchas to resolve their problem bypassing the tantric.

At night the sky was clear and everything around were clearly visible in bright moon light. The Sherpa assistants of the Lama had gone back to their village. The Lama took Nil and Doma along to visit the caves. Two large caves were arranged for the stay of Doma and Nil respectively. They were not far from the largest cave where the Lama himself resided. There were six other caves as storehouses, kitchen and for temporary shelter of the villagers. All these caves had been recently carved out by the villagers. The sacred caves were higher up in the hill. They were made for sacred meditation and ordinary people were not permitted to visit them except at the time of Buddhist festivals.

They had to climb a steep causeway to reach the sacred caves amidst pines, rhododendrons and flowery bushes. Doma helped Nil to climb up the rise. Nil was enchanted to watch the semicircular caves curved dexterously into the hard stony wall of the hill. They first entered the main cave. It was about fifteen feet wide and twenty feet in length. The roof was semi-circular and at the middle it was about fifteen feet from the floor laden with granite sheets. At the far end of the cave there was a large Buddha statue of snow white marble about ten feet tall. There were bas relieves of various Hindu gods and goddesses immaculately set on the walls. There were five smaller caves on either side of the main cave and each of them was painted with Jataka stories of Bodhisatva (Buddha in earlier births). After visiting the caves they climbed down for dinner. Thereafter in the moonlit night in front of the residential caves

the Lama told them the history of the sacred caves. Nobody in fact could know the exact time of creation of these caves. In a sacred Pali text in birch barks, a brief account of the caves was written. The text was preserved in an ancient monastery at Sikkim. The Lamas of these caves were appointed by the monastery and he had to read the sacred scripture before taking charge of these caves. This Lama called Samten had learnt the history from the sacred text at Sikkim. This cannot be disclosed to any ordinary persons but these two being divine persons Samten did not hesitate to tell them the history.

King Bimbisar of the ancient Indian kingdom of Magadha was an ardent devotee of Lord Buddha and he had made many monasteries in his state and always sponsored the Buddhist religion. Unfortunately his son Ajatasatru (495-462 B.C.) was a dogmatic Hindu and hated the Buddhists. To escape from his wrath a few Buddhist monks escaped into these hills and started residing in the caves. Around 254 B.C. during the reign of the Mauryan Emperor Asoka who used to patronize the Buddhists, relation of the monks at the caves with Magadha was reestablished and Granites and Marble stones and sculptors were sent from Magadha to curve statues and images of Lord Buddha and Jataka stories. The history of the caves in the holy book was written till the early Gupta era as the last page of the text mentioned the visit of the king Samudra Gupta. Thereafter nothing could be known about the caves. Some natural disaster could have isolated the caves from the outside world and because of lack of food, the monks might have died. The caves were rediscovered during the 8th century A.D. while Guru Rinpoche (Padmasambhava) introduced Buddhism among the hill people of Bhutan and Sikkim (Darjeeling hills and these caves belonged to Sikkim at that time).

Rinpoche had decided to meditate at a secret place away from the Sherpa and Bhutia villages. So he preferred the jungles in the slopes of the adjacent hills. Two of his trusted disciples suddenly came upon the gumphas (Buddhist caves) hidden under deep jungles. Rinpoche thought them to be the gift from heaven and slowly cleared the caves and started meditating there. He declared that none except himself and his two best disciples would have the right to visit the caves. Any trespasser would be punished by divine power. He chose the place for his secret meditation. However, replicas of the gumphas were

created at the bottom of the hill for commoners. Inside the cave he discovered skeletons of the Lamas who had died long ago and some sacred texts written on birch barks one of which depicted the history of the caves. He left the place after some time entrusting one of his trusted disciples to look after the sacred caves. He took along most of the sacred texts found in the caves except one that depicted the history of

the caves. The tradition of appointing a new young Lama directly from Tibet, after the death of each

Lama, continued until Tibet was taken over by China during the middle of the twentieth century. Most of

the sacred Lamas then fled and took shelter in monasteries at Sikkim. Thereafter the Lamas of the sacred caves were being appointed by the Sikkim monasteries.

Chapter 7: The Plan

Nil was fully recovered now, but he still felt too weak to climb steep hills. So Samten advised them to wait a few days more. In the mean time they could chalk out the plan to reach the cursed plateau from this side without alerting the tantric's men. It was not a simple task. There were no clear tracks to reach the plateau from this side. It was situated above a high hill about thousand feet from here and this side of the hill was covered with dense forest. The summit of the hill was almost flat and extended up to the bottom

of the cursed plateau. The place was covered with tall trees and invisible from the top of the plateau. So their task would be to first cut out a path to reach the top of this hill. This should be done at night to avoid curiosity of the villagers. Then they should make a temporary shelter at the flat crest of the hill. The plateau was barely two hundred feet from there and the slope was gentle. But the last part of the task, to curve out a path to the plateau would not be simple. Men of the tantric were sure to guard the place and any noise might attract their attention. And if they were detected the mission would be spoilt.

After one week Nil was perfectly fit for the adventure, and he and Doma planned to begin the first part of their scheme at night. The steep rise of thousand feet leading to the level spot at the approach to

the plateau was covered with tall trees and bushes. The bushes between adjacent tall trees could be cleared to cut out a path to reach the saddle point where the gentle rise to the plateau began. The climb would not be very difficult if the path cut was a zigzag with moderate slope and the adjacent trees would also help as support at the time of climbing. The path cut in this way would be about thousand and five hundred feet and if they could cut out hundred and fifty feet a day, it would be complete by ten to twelve days. The snakes, leeches and noxious insects were likely to be hiding inside the bushes. So they should be well guarded against these hazards. They would have to complete every day's work at night but it would not be safe to carry lights which could be seen from a distance and might raise curiosity in the minds of the villagers. However, the forest was not dense enough to block entry of moonlight. So they won't have to work in complete darkness if they started their work a few days before the full moon. Then on the next

new moon night they would explore the cursed plateau under cover of darkness.

Nil and Doma presented the plan to Samten and discussed the prose and cons of their project with him. Samten was highly satisfied with the plan and approved it immediately. He prayed to Lord Buddha for success of their mission. They at last decided to start the work on the eleventh day after the new moon.

On the crucial day they meditated for some time in the afternoon and started cutting off the bushes at

7 p.m. They planned to cut out the path in the rightward direction so that the intensity of the steep slope was lessened. However this would increase the distance of the target as compared to the straight climb but climbing would be easier now. To enable free movement both of them wore pants and shirts and their gumboot reached almost their knees. The long boots had spikes at the bottom. These boots would be helpful to protect them from leeches, noxious insects and even snakes. They took long clubs to beat down the bushes and frighten away the inmates. The inward side of the sticks were affixed with cotton soaked

in salt water. This would be necessary to clear off the leeches in case they happened to get into their bodies in spite of the protections. They smeared their faces and hands with mosquito oil to escape the onslaught of the gnats and mosquitoes. As the gaps between the trees were not uniform the path they cut off zigzagged like the letter 's'. Moonlight now reached them through the gaps at tops of the trees and swaying of the braches above started casting flickering shadows and they were engulfed in an uncanny ambience. The bushes ahead looked like dark monsters. At places the gaps were uniform permitting them to cut off a straight path up to some distance and it looked like a narrow tunnel with walls of bushes on either side. At first Doma started cutting off the bushes with the sharp chopper and behind her Nil throwing away the debris on either side of the path. After a while the tasks were interchanged and in this way they cleared off about seventy feet to reach a level spot where the trees were sparse.

They cleared off a circular patch and sat down to rest for a while. The moon was now distinctly visible through the opening above and everything appeared mystic and dreamy to Nil. They were now drenched in sweat and both of them put off their shirts to dry them. Nil looked away from Doma who was now with only the lacy bra unraveling her large and well formed boobs. Doma started giggling loudly raising echoes all around at the embarrassment of Nil who turned sideways to avoid her passionate countenance burning with deep desire. Nil prayed to god to give him power to overcome the outburst of passion simmering within. Doma might not be very serious about the maintenance of sanctity for success of the mission or god might be testing through her Nil's mental power to overcome temptation.

Nil collected himself and looked straight into her eyes. She moved forward toward him and caught hold of his shoulders hard and bent forward now fully unraveling the throbbing boobs and her eyes were burning with uncontrollable desire. Nil said in an icy voice, 'let's put on our garments and resume work.' Doma stepped back glumly and turned her head to hide the tears dripping down her ruddy cheeks.

Nil felt sorry for her and said in a placatory voice, 'we are but ordinary humans and the divinity assigned on us by people has not yet shown any manifestation. So we ought to be careful about outbursts of passion. Sex for ordinary men is simply a vice unless specifically targeted at procreation. So during sacred missions even married couples are to abstain from physical union. In a higher level of yogic achievement, however, as in the case of a true tantric, sex is the counter part of the cosmic union between the 'purusha', the supreme stable force and 'prakriti', or 'shakti' the feminine counterpart, the supreme mother god creating this palpable universe. But unless a couple transcends through to the level at which they visualize their identity with the cosmic power, they should always treat sex as a transitory means to gratify lust unless specifically intended to have children and therefore it should be avoided in all auspicious pursuits. Now we are in a sacred mission and we are still ordinary humans and therefore we should be cautious not to indulge in passions.'

Doma raised her eyes and looked admiringly at Nil. It seemed she was highly impressed by his wisdom. She said in a tone like an obedient school student,

'I'm very much impressed by your discourse but as it was very brief I could not comprehend the essence of your mystic suggestions. Will you please explain in detail the essence of tantric cult? This would also be helpful for me to understand fully the designs of this mysterious tantric here.'

Nil replied, 'my knowledge in this arena is but superficial. I'll tell you whatever I know about this esoteric cult, but that too would take time. So let's first finish today's target and thereafter we would have time enough to discuss the matter.'

She soon got down to business. They completed the targeted work by two more hours. Getting back to the caves they took some rest and thereafter got out and seated at the edge of the hillock and Nil unraveled to Doma the mystery of the tantric cult, its superiority over other forms of mystic cult and also the grave danger associated with it.

Doma listened to him patiently and assured him that she would now forget everything and concentrate only on the mission. Then she suddenly turned morose and said with a forced smile, 'I know you'd leave me after completion of the mission and get back to your place.'

She could not hold her tears. Nil consoled her in an emotional voice, 'trust me, I promise never to leave you.'

Doma glanced at Nil with ecstatic eyes and then blushed and moved away to hide her embarrassment.

Chapter 8: The Promise

Nil got perturbed as he remembered his promise to goddess Kali in his dream that he would not get mixed up with this divine girl. But it would not be an easy task. Behavior of Doma so far indicated that

she had lost all patience and her desire for Nil had been intensifying day by day. Apparently his wise talks on the need of abstinence was convincing to Doma but Nil knew well that all his theoretical convictions would be swept away if the tornado of repressed passions broke through the barriers of taboos.

This was true for both Nil and Doma. Both were repressing their innate desires for each other. He apprehended their proximity would soon shatter all their vows and this meant spoiling the mission. She had been strongly drawn to him from the very moment of rescuing him from the snow storm. Nil too had felt uncontrollable desire for her even before he had seen her. Now he felt honestly that contrary to all his wistful tall talks to Doma he at heart desired her strongly and his desire was intensifying day by day by Doma's insinuating behavior. The repressed passion was simmering within and at any weak moment it may shatter all his resistance.

They could however, restrain themselves with strong will power till completion of the mission, but thereafter he would have to keep his promise to Doma. She restrained herself now being assured by the promise and it would be disastrous for her if he went back on the promise after completion of the mission. Nil's head got jumbled and he could not think any more over the tricky matter. They returned to the caves at midnight and he was relieved to find her hilarious. All the way back, she had no longer made any insinuating gestures and looked like a sacred goddess. The promise must have done it. Nil decided to concentrate on the immediate task alone and not to dwell any more upon the promise till completion of

the mission.

On the second day, they started at the same time as the day before and now they cut out the track in the leftward direction to keep at the center of the spot right beneath the plateau. Doma was completely different now, jolly and in a dancing mood. It was the effect of the promise, Nil thought and this made him guilt conscious thinking of the uncertain future of the promise. In this part the tops of the trees were closer permitting lesser moon light and the semi dark ambience appeared spooky. The atmosphere reverberated with monotonous sharp noise made by the crickets. It appeared as though someone was relentlessly ringing a temple bell. Nil was possessed with an eerie sensation of invisible eyes keeping constant watch on them. Rodents scurried off and insects and nocturnal birds fluttered away as they started cutting off the bushes mercilessly.

Suddenly Nil noticed some leeches on the bare arm of Doma. He immediately brushed them off by the salted cotton on his stick. Blood was oozing out of the place of attack. Doma started giggling and collecting an herb from the bushes she administered the paste of the leaves on the injury and bleeding stopped immediately. 'Oh, they had been feeding on my blood for such a long time and I could not feel

it.' She said and once again burst out giggling. Nil explained to her that the leeches pour out an anesthetic before attacking the body of an animal and because of the numbness caused by the liquid the victim cannot feel the attack.

After some time they discovered a water course. The bottom was about ten feet wide and free from bushes and shrubs. It was dry now and could be used as a track. They followed the course of the channel which had gone upwards in the leftward direction first and then taken a circular turn to the right. At last it ended up in a large pit. This was much helpful for them as they could finish their targeted task earlier. While resting at the last point of their path Doma started humming a joyous song, the language of which was alien to Nil, but the tune was charming. It was perfectly in harmony with the murmur of the leaves of the trees above. At Nil's request she raised her voice and the ambience was saturated with the melody. Thereafter they gossiped for some time and on the way back Nil inadvertently stepped on a boulder inside the water course and got a bruise at his left ankle. It was not very serious but Nil had a limp during the

rest of the return. Returning to the caves, Doma rubbed his ankle with herbal oil and asked him to take rest the next day. But next morning there was no trace of the sprain and Nil decided to continue work as he was perfectly fit.

Chapter 9: Temptation

Next morning Nil was perturbed to hear Namsell talking with Samten in an unintelligible dialect. He did not come out of the cave but he was already familiar with the voice of Namsell. The reply of Samten was laconic and at last he said something gruffly after which Namsell left. So Namsell was still after them

and Nil was sure he had some evil design – likely to be spying on them and trying to find out what he and Doma were after. It was clear to Nil that the man did not buy their story of high level meditation in the caves. Nil was a bit perturbed. If Namsell went on spying it would be impossible to carry on their mission secretly. It was highly likely that he would roam around at night too. When Samten met then to learn about the progress of the day's work he informed Nil that Namsell was querying about them and he had told him gruffly that it was sacrilegious on the part of common people to have curiosity about high level

religious monks and nuns. Samten too suspected Namsell to have something to do with the tantric. He had already gathered information that the man frequently visited the tantric's temple and also practiced tantra cult. It was quite likely that he was an informer appointed by the tantric.

While Nil expressed his apprehensions that if the man spied on them at night too, it would be impossible to keep their mission secret from the tantric. He also informed Samten in detail how the Bhutia had followed him right from his arrival at the New Jalpaiguri railway station. At this Samten smiled and said that the man had never been to the plains to the best of his knowledge. He assured Nil that he had forbidden Namsell to enter the sacred place again and his trusted men were keeping strict watch on the movements of Namsell. Nil, however, could not shake the disquiet off his mind all through the day.

But he forgot it when they started work in the evening. Doma was now completely transformed. She looked jovial and enthusiastic, but never made any insinuating gesture, nor did she look at Nil with lustful eyes. The promise had done the miracle, Nil thought. But he was very much confused at the complicated nature of his thought process. While she had been trying to tempt him into sin, he was extremely worried and prayed to god to give him power to overcome temptation. So, her behavior now should have satisfied him. But, instead, something started pinching him. Her apathetic attitude toward him made him feel

lonely and hollow. So, notwithstanding outward exhortations to maintain perfect sanctity, did his subconscious mind rejoice her outburst of passion? He said to himself, 'do I really desire in my inner mind that she reveals her strong desire and lust toward me? How funny! While she expresses her strong desire for me I feel perturbed, but if she behaves the other way, I feel morose and abandoned.'

They worked hard for the next few days and their progress was uninterrupted and completely free from hazards and they could reach the targeted spot two days before the estimated time. The hilly path rose steeply and then ended into a level ground about thirty feet long and twenty five feet wide. The trees were sparse here. The level ground ended in a gentle slope climbing the cursed plateau. Everything was clearly visible in bright moon light. They hastened to cut off the bushes and clear a large circular space. They closely inspected the spot and the adjacent rise of the plateau and there was no indication that the place had been visited by any human being in near past. So it would be a safe hiding place and a base

from where they could venture into the plateau. They would undertake the first venture under the cover of darkness. The outside temple with the humanoid image of the goddess was for the ordinary devotees. The tantric rituals must be performed at a secret place. They would have to trace it out without being detected by the tantric and his men.

With the twigs of the pines and strong creepers and using the tree trunks as poles they started erecting three shanties – one for Nil, the second for Doma and the small one as kitchen and store room. They used tarpaulin and mats as the roofs. In three days the temporary shelter was erected. The gaps between trees being irregularly spaced the roofs of the shanties took odd shapes raising laughter of both Nil and Doma.

On the fourth day, they moved on to their new home. It was very thrilling for them. Doma was very hilarious and always crooning songs in her own dialect. She inaugurated their new life by preparing spice-tea in her new kitchen.

She said in a light mood, 'after completion of the mission we won't go back to the localities and live in this beautiful house'.

Nil said, 'but this makeshift shanty won't withstand strong wind or rain'

'We shall make it stronger later on' Doma replied forthright.

Nil felt pricks inside. Doma had taken his promise seriously and taken it for granted that they would marry and live together after completion of the mission, but it appeared absurd to Nil.

Nil felt at his heart that sooner or later all her dreams would be completely shattered and the rest of the lives of both of them would be miserable and tragic. Nil went out of the room under the ruse of inspecting the creeper bindings of the structure simply to conceal his emotions. 'No, I should ignore these worries and be solely preoccupied with the sacred mission now,' Nil said to himself.

The moon went down behind the hills soon and it was dark only with the cluster of stars in the clear sky. The ambience with the dark hills and trees around and the sky dotted with stars enchanted Nil. The crickets were making their monotonous noises, interrupted occasionally by sounds of insects and screeches of nocturnal birds. They started their adventure toward the plateau and Nil's heart throbbed with thrill and consternation. Doma's face in semi darkness looked uncanny. She was now preoccupied only with the adventure.

The slope was gentle and the bushes sparse and they could effortlessly climb upwards keeping to the middle of the plateau. Soon they came upon a clear space with only the scattered burnt trunks of trees. Nil realized that these were the leftover of the ominous conflagration. They moved very cautiously making least possible noise and keeping strict watch on all sides. The causeway leading to the temple and the top of the plateau was now only a few feet from them. The silhouette of the dome of the temple with flags at the top was now clearly visible. Nil's heartbeats increased in excitement. They were soon going to enter the forbidden zone and henceforth they would have to be very cautious. The causeway leading to the temple went further up to enter the forbidden zone and devotees were not permitted to move beyond the temple. They decided to return now and continue the venture the next day. On their return they fortunately came upon a depressed spot from where they could keep watch on the causeway remaining under the

cover of the burnt trunks guarding the front of the low land.

They returned to the shanty and Doma lighted the stove to prepare the dinner. In bed confused thoughts and contradictory emotions streamed through Nil's mind. He at times felt that his promise to the goddess was simply a dream. So nothing harmful would come out of their physical union. Then his thoughts drifted to the tantric. All the promises of the tantric to the hill people appeared to be sheer hype to Nil and he guessed that all the hazards of the hill people were but designs of the tantric.

He now felt happy that the thought of the tantric had helped him overcome temptations and he had passed the first of the stringent tests he was put into by the goddess.

Chapter 10: The Tantric's Cave

The next day they came to their shanty at late noon and after tea, they proceeded for the hideout behind the burnt tree trunks. Darkness was just falling and the atmosphere was filled with a fine layer of fog and it was a bit chilly.

From behind the tree trunk they watched the causeway to the temple for some time and there was no sign of anybody moving along. They came out of the hiding and proceeded carefully toward the causeway. The path was cut by footsteps in between thick velvety grasses. Small trees and bushes had grown up on both the sides and they were shaped into orderly fencing. They soon reached the spot where the path was bifurcated, the left one leading to the stairs of the temple. The temple was now clearly in sight as the sky was free from clouds. The central structure of the temple was about twelve feet high with a conical narrow turret with a trident at the top. The temple was made of unpolished pinewood logs on poles about four feet high. Wooden stairs led to a verandah about three feet wide and at the end of the

verandah there was a small door which was locked now. They, however, had no interest in the temple and took to the other track that climbed a bit steeply to the right. The narrow track to the right was fenced on both sides with thorny shrubs. Doma cautioned Nil, 'be careful about the thorns. They are very poisonous and may even cause death.' So they moved along very cautiously. There was, however, no sign of any movement or sounds above. After some time they had to stop in front of a locked wooden gate about six feet high with sharp nails at the top. The thorny plants were taller on both sides of the gate and there was no way to cross the gate. Through the slits of the logs of the gate they had a glance of the track inside

which had cut deep into the body of the hill and curved down into a narrow cave with a circular mouth about four feet in diameter. It was all dark inside and nothing beyond was visible. They guessed that the cave could be entered only by going on all fours.

Standing helplessly at the gate they could not make out what to do next. They agreed at last that the forbidden zone could not be invaded from this side and hey would have to explore an alternative approach to the cave. Now it was clear to them that the approach to the plateau must be through the cave and to reach the top of the plateau, they would have to reach the cave by some means. At many places, on the return path, the thorny bush was narrow and shorter. But if they tried to cut them off at any place here, it would for sure come to the notice of the tantric's men or visitors of the temple. So, they had no alternative but to explore some alternative path from some other place away from the causeway to the temple.

Doma said enthusiastically, 'I've marked the location of the cave and inspected all its sides. It could easily be approached from the right side. What we are to do now is to walk to the north of the hiding place and find out some suitable place to climb up to the northern side of the cave and thereafter we could easily get to the mouth of the cave.'

Nil said in a dubious tone, 'are you sure we could reach the cave from the other side?'

'Cheer up and have trust on me. By tomorrow, we are sure to reach the cave.'

'But it would take time. Do you like to explore the alternative right now?'

'I think it would be better to return to the shanty now and explore the alternative tomorrow after chalking out a new plan.'

Nil agreed with her and they returned to the shanty and Doma got busy preparing dinner.

The dinner with chowmin and chilly sauce was delicious and Nil, being very hungry, devoured it with relish. He was tired too and fell fast asleep as soon as he went to bed. Suddenly he felt something pressing him hard and streams of hot blood rushed to his head as he discovered the nude body of Doma embracing him hard, her soft boobs pressing against his chest and tongue trying to open his mouth. Her hand played down his body, unlaced the pajama and reached for the hardness, he promptly took her

tongue into his mouth, moved his hand on to her butts and drew her madly toward him and his sleep broke off and he felt the coldness of the wet underwear between his legs. Nil felt ashamed of the dream which was nothing but the outburst of his repressed longings.

He started arguing out and at last came to the conviction that there was no fault in desiring Doma and he could not resist temptation to please his eyes with the view of her sleeping body. He moved close to

the curtain and peeped through the raised corner. She was sleeping peacefully with her hands resting on her open boobs and the chiaroscuro, made by the scanty moon rays through the slits of the tarpaulin roof, created a mystic aura around her. Her tousled hair were spread around the pillow and with her lips half open, she looked like a voluptuous nymph. How long could he resist the temptation? It was not at all necessary to attach any importance to his promise in dream to the goddess, but he could no longer make the first move as he had dissuaded her while she was burning with passion. But if there be any more insinuating gesture on her part he would not hesitate a moment to get their mutual desire fulfilled. He would have to wait till that moment and it appeared unendurable to him. The hardness tormenting him and he had to relieve the agony by jacking off. As soon as he was relieved shame and moroseness took possession of him and he felt contrite for his erotic thoughts.

The next morning unexpected information from Doma like bolt from the blue made Nil extremely disappointed and perturbed. She took him aside after their talks about the plan of the next part of the venture, and disclosed the fact after long hesitation and blushing that she had got approval from her parents of their marriage after completion of the mission. Samten and the Lama at the village had already approved it. In fact all of them taken it for granted from the very beginning that Nil and Doma were drawn to each other and would marry in future. They had considered it to be a pious union between two divine souls. After Nil's promise to fulfill her desire a few days ago, she needed permission from her parents and the religious chiefs. Now she had got all these and there was no obstacle on the path of their union for life after the mission.

Both of them remained silent for some time. Doma broke the silence and said enthusiastically,

'I've also taken up a Hindu brata learnt from a Nepali housewife. You must know this ritual performed by betrothed Hindu maidens for the wellbeing of would be husbands and success of their marriage.'

Nil forced a smile and said, 'yes I know the brata. A maiden undertaking this brata vows to god that she would remain pure and would not indulge in any sexual relation with the beloved until they are married. During this period she is to remove all physical desires for the beloved from her mind.'

'Exactly and this would be very helpful for the success of our mission.' Doma looked proud and ebullient.

Nil felt morose and abandoned. With utmost efforts he collected himself and said, 'you have unquestionably done a judicious job with perfect foresight.'

He felt his head reeling and hollow within. He left her alone under the ruse of some important task. Doma entered her cave jubilantly and got settled to her prayer which was an important part of the brata. Nil walked to the corner of the hill. He had to be alone for some time to get accustomed to the onslaught that had just befallen him. He felt vehement turmoil within and his mind became puzzled, unable to think any further. He had given up smoking for a long time but a few packs were stored in his bag. He went to the cave and came back with a pack of cigarettes and the lighter and went on smoking one after another. All his inner cravings for transitory union with her had now been shattered. But the most serious problem was how to escape from this place after the mission. It was no longer confined between him and Doma. All the hill people had now taken it for granted that he and Doma were going to marry after the mission. How could he leave the place escaping from the notice of the hill people? The way out from the region was not easy and he would certainly be caught on the way and punished if he attempted to flee without marrying her.

Nil thought carefully about marriage and his mind revolted. He felt that he loved her spontaneously and for sure it was his first genuine love. He had never loved Sima. It was simply affection due to familiarity from very childhood. But he loved Doma seriously and he was still deeply desirous of physical union with her. But marriage was something different. This would imply either he would have to live here with the hill people or Doma would have to relocate to Calcutta. Either of this would be disastrous for

both of them and soon their love would dissipate. He could not marry Doma and nor would he be able marry any other girl and would have to remain a bachelor till his dying day with the memory of Doma. The same would be the case for Doma. Both of them would be unhappy at this but their love would remain alive and sacred. But marriage would be something horrible, making them unhappy with mutual hatred.

He now sincerely appreciated Doma for her decision to undergo the brata. Physical union without marriage would be nothing but deceiving Doma and a grave sin, generating hatred in her for him, and his lifelong prick of conscience. Momentary pleasure would for sure lead to pernicious consequences for the future. He felt now that she had saved him by taking up the brata. So now the crucial question was how to escape after completion of the mission or would it at all be possible for him to escape? Even if he abandoned the mission and tried to escape, he would be caught on the way. Escaping from this isolated hilly place without being detected was impossible. He felt it was meaningless to ponder over this tricky problem and no solution would come out by racking his brains. So it was better to surrender himself to fate and give his best possible efforts for the mission.

Nil's father used to say that when one is in a serious dilemma and cannot make out what to do, the best alternative is to stop thinking and worrying and to surrender oneself completely to God or any deity he has faith in and divine power would resolve the problem. Being in an impasse, Nil followed his father's advice and surrendered himself unconditionally to God and in a moment all his worries and disquiet of mind vanished. His peace of mind returned and he remembered the sloka of Gita his father used to recite and explain. It was a gospel of Lord Krishna to the Pandava warrior Arjuna. The essence of the sloka is that a person has right over his works and duties but no right or control over the outcome. So one should concentrate on his duties and perform them in the best possible manner without worrying about the results as he had neither command nor any right over the results. So Nil decided to go ahead

with the noble duty, entrusted to him, in the best possible manner without the slightest deviation from it. He would now concentrate on the immediate tasks relevant to the mission, i.e. to discover the alternative path to the mouth of the cave and forget the trifles like his relation with Doma and its future. He threw away the butt of the last cigarette of the packet and returned to his cave with perfect peace and equanimity of mind. Doma was standing at the entrance of the cave and said jovially, 'where had you been so long? I have been looking for you for a long time to show you the sketch of the plan for today's adventure.'

'Oh, I sat at the corner of the hill to the south and enjoying the hide and seek game of the clouds and the hills.'

'You are a crazy boy!' Doma said in the tone of a loving mother. 'Anyway, it's almost lunch time. Come right to my cave with me.'

Nil followed her calmly to her cave. She spread a sheet of paper on a raised platform of stone at the corner of the cave and highlighted the sketch depicted on it by torch light. It was a picture of the bottom of the plateau, neatly drawn in black pencil and their hideout and some other important spots marked out by red color. She pointed her right index finger to a red-marked spot to the north of their hideout and said that it could be the likely spot from where they would start climbing in quest of the alternative path to the cave-mouth. She had also sketched the expected path to the desired point of climbing, but she said that

they would have to alter it according to the real situation. The spot was away from the point just below the cave and therefore they should follow a climbing path that would bend to the left so as to converge to the cave. Nil was very much impressed by the plan and was amazed at the sense of geography and geometry

of the uneducated hill girl.

After discussing the plan and necessary things to be carried with them for the venture, Doma went to the small kitchen inside the cave and got busy arranging the lunch. She announced that she had a pleasant surprise for Nil who was really astounded and got immense pleasure to find the lunch menu of boiled rice, Bengali style potato curry and daal. He ate with relish as he got the savor of Bengali food after a long

time. Doma was also taking the same food like one perfectly accustomed to Bengali food.

Nil asked her in a an astonished voice, 'where have you learnt cooking Bengali dishes from?

'Magic,' Doma started giggling.

'Be serious Doma. However, you have every right to keep it from me.'

'Oh my god the little boy has turned sentimental!' She giggled again.

'Close to our village, there's a Nepali settlement' she continued, 'and the Nepali girls likes me very much. Mina Chhetri, a Nepali housewife, who had been to Siliguri where her husband worked at a hotel, has taught me Bengali cooking. The brata, too, I've learnt from Mina.'

'Have you learnt from her any Bengali words?'

'Only a few.'

'I like to hear them from your mouth.'

'Okay' she started giggling and said 'the words I've learnt are: ami tomake bhalobasi (I love you).' Doma ran away giggling.

They reached the hiding place before sunset. According to the plan they started moving rightward targeting the specific spot from where they were to start climbing. Lumps of clouds were moving incessantly across the sky. They were purely cirrus and therefore there was no possibility of rain but as they obstructed the natural light after sunset, it soon became dark. The hillside now was not as gently sloped as in the place where they had scaled up to the hiding. It was now steeper and shorn of burnt tree trunks. They had to move very carefully in the darkness watching out each step. Fortunately, there were projections from hill to catch hold of and they moved along these narrow risky path, sometimes climbing upwards and sometimes downwards. They reached the spot from where to climb as highlighted in the sketch, but the hill had an inward inclination and so it was impossible to climb upwards from this spot. They had already moved about fifty feet away from the point right beneath the cave-mouth. So any further northward movement meant moving further away from the cave. But there was no alternative. So they went on walking further to the north and found that the hill had taken a circular right turn after which the upward slope was very gentle.

It became very dark and they had to switch on the torches suspended from their necks by threads. The place was under the cover of the hill and there was no possibility of anyone seeing the torch light from above the plateau. Now the hillside was easy to climb and they went on climbing upward in the leftward direction. Soon they came upon a narrow dry water course about three feet wide. It was semi-elliptical. They reached the curve and found that the water course had cut into the body of the hill and gone upwards with gentle slope in the rightward direction. So, if they followed the water course they would move

further away from the cave. But scaling upwards at this place straight or in the leftward direction was almost impossible, especially in this darkness. So they decided to follow the water course and see where it led them to.

The heights of the walls on both sides went on increasing and eventually they discovered themselves inside a tunnel, which was wider and easy to walk along. The tunnel in front had sloped steeply down and because of overhanging bushes from either wall, it was pitch dark. Nil focused the torch ahead and guessed that the tunnel had bifurcated at about ten feet from them. They agreed that if they took the leftward tunnel there would be a fair chance to get closer to the tantric's cave. The tunnel ahead was overgrown with mosses and weeds and this indicated that it was not visited by anybody for a long time. They beat down the bushes and tore with their long sticks the creeper roofing to let moonlight in. Getting close to the bifurcation they turned left and soon ended up at a depressed large rectangular ground. It was like a pond about ten feet deep. Focusing his torch into the pond Nil uttered a shriek of panic and drew back. Doma snatched the torch from his shaking hand. She too got startled as soon as she glanced into the pond.. Then collecting themselves from the first shock they looked into the pond closely. It was filled

with human skulls and bones. There was no way to go any further and they returned to the bifurcation. They would have to explore the rightward tunnel. They felt exhausted and decided to get back to the caves next morning and continue the venture after discussing the skull issue with Samten.

Chapter 11: Tantra Mystery

The skeletons and the skulls they had discovered convinced Nil, Doma and Samten that the tantric worshipped the goddess with human sacrifice. Nil felt it necessary before further adventure to get some more information about the tantric from the guru at Tarapith. So he left for Darjeeling alone. Samten had given him an address of a reliable Sherpa near the Victoria Falls at Darjeeling. When Nil called at his house the man gladly received Nil without any query. After some rest he went to the mall and from a cyber cafe emailed to Shyamal informing him about everything and also asking him to meet the guru immediately and gather detail information of the tantric here.

Going out of the cafe he opened his cell phone and found the battery down. He turned around to look for the recharging pluck and was panicked to find Namsell quickly receding into a lane. Then he had even come to Darjeeling to espy him? 'No I can't prevent him. I should not waste time on him any more. Let him do whatever he likes. I should only be cautious,' Nil said to himself and recharged the battery from a call center and called Shyamal standing at a clear spot so that the Bhutia could not be at audible distance without being noticed. Nil asked Shyamal to read his email and reply immediately. Shyamal sent an sms that he would meet the guru soon and email back the next day. So Nil had to stay at Darjeeling for one more day. Next day he got the email with an attachment. He opened it and asked the cyber owner to give him a printout of the text. He deleted the file before leaving. He took the printout and after meeting the Sherpa left Darjeeling and reached the caves in the evening after two days.

Next morning Nil invited Doma to his cave and started reading the emailed text The printout was about thirty five pages giving details about tantra cult and the background of this tantric. Nil read the text with rapt attention and after reading each paragraph he explained the contents to Doma and thereafter they openly discussed the matters and in this way they could have a clear insight into the mystic cult of tantra.

No body could tell when the tantra cult originated. It appeared as a parallel to Hatha-Yogic cult which contained similar physiological postures and breathing exercises and also the ultimate goal of self

realization and unification with the supreme was the same. But they differed radically as regards the approach towards our desires, emotions and passions, especially those pertaining to food and sex habits. Yoga cult considered all our physical desires as vices and suggested repression and abstention from the very beginning. On the other hand tantra cult considered our worldly desires as natural and endowed us by god. They are vices so long as they remain crude and confined to transitory gratification of desires. So the tantric recognizes them as reality and without repressing them he is to be taboo-free about all desires for sex and food. His endeavor should be to transcend the crude aspect and get all these desires sublimated to

a higher plain. In this way sex ultimately transcends to a level where the physical union of the male and the female transcends to the cosmic union of 'purusha' and 'prakriti'.

The first evidence of these esoteric cults dates back to about 5000 B.C. Sculptures of yogic postures have been discovered in excavations pertaining to Indus valley civilization. The first literary evidence of esoteric cult is Atharva Veda which is not considered as pious by the orthodox Vedic school. However, the magic and charms depicted in Atharva Veda are considerably different from the tantric practices. Later on tantric cult evolved and took various forms under Vazrajan and Zen schools of Buddhism, and Sakta, Vaishnab and Saiba schools of Hinduism. During the fifteenth century the Hath Yoga cult was rejuvenated by borrowing heavily from the physical rites of tantra.

The rigorous tantra cult of the Sakta school is popularly known as tantrism in India. This school belongs to the vamachari Sakta cult. Their descriptions of inner human anatomy and physiology are the closest to modern bio-scientific discoveries of human economy. The tantra cult developed in course of millennia long trial and error but the tantrics had no scientific theoretical knowledge and so they mixed up mysticism and extra mundane speculative philosophy with tantra. Their goal too was mystic, to resolve

the mystery of life and death and union with the creator of the universe.

Tantra cult describes seven chakras (wheels) in human body. Their locations are: coccyx (muladhar chakra), sacrum (swadhisthan chakra), lumbar close to the navel (manipur chakra), thoracic close to the heart (anahata chakra), cervical close to the throat (visuddha chakra), base of the scull in between the angle of the eyes and the pituitary gland (ajna chakra) and top of the cerebrum (sahasrar chakra).

These chakras rest at important nerve plexuses, major points of contact between the central, sympathetic and parasympathetic nervous systems and some major endocrine glands.

Tantrics like the yogis believe that our main source of life force and vital energy is stored in a dormant form in the coccyx. They get this shrouded in mystery by visualizing that goddess kundalini as the source of our life force lies dormant in the coccyx in three and a half fold coil.

In fact this is nothing but our life force in the form of genetic code of the DNA. For ordinary persons only an insignificant fraction of the genetic potential become manifest. Moreover the coccyx region is one of the two most important feedback centers (the other is at the top of the cerebrum) for the central and autonomic (sympathetic and parasympathetic) nervous systems.

Central nervous system relates to our conscious knowledge. But most of the vital functions are performed without our conscious knowledge by the autonomic nervous systems. They are like an extremely powerful computer mechanism with programs embedded in the genetic code. For ordinary persons only a tiny fraction of these programs are operative.

The tantric rites through breathing control and auto suggestions endeavor to retrieve from the hard disc stored in the coccyx the dormant genetic potentials. They, however, define this as awakening of the kundalini goddess, the supreme mother goddess responsible for giving shape to the palpable universe and the energies that flow through this universe. She is lying dormant in three and a half coil inside the muladhar chakra. We are to wake her and let her move upwards along the path of the chakras toward the sahasrar chakra at the top of the cerebrum where the supreme god 'purusha' (the inert and invisible creator by whose command and will the supreme mother goddess has created this visible universe) resides. With the ascent of the mother goddess along the path defined by the chakras the tantric acquires extra ordinary supernatural powers and ultimately if the goddess can get untied with the supreme god at sahasrar, the tantric becomes one with the supreme and gets free from the cycle of birth and death.

The tantrics or yogis learnt about the immense power that could be acquired by complicated postures and breathing exercises and meditation through millennia long trial and error process. Without any scientific knowledge, they ascribed this to be the manifestation of power of the goddess kundalini who after being awakened moves upwards with continued efforts of the tantric and higher and higher she moves the man is endowed with more and more spectacular powers.

Breathing processes (pranayam) and mudras (complicated yogic postures) are very crucial to the awakening of the kundalini. The breathing tracks are called nadis (rivers). Three rivers are visualized by tantric cult. All the rivers originate at the coccyx and end up at the top of the cerebrum. The first river 'Ida' starts from the left side and the second river 'pingala' begins at the right side of the coccyx. They alternate sides by crossing each chakra. Ida touches the left nostril after crossing the visuddha chakra and gets connected with inhalation through the left nostril and thereafter crosses the ajna chakra to reach the sahasrar chakra from the right side. Pingala, on the other hand, follows an opposite course, gets entangled with breathing through the right nostril and ends up at the left side of the sahasrar. Beginning at the

coccyx like the other two the central river susumna crosses ida and pingala at each chakra and eventually meets with them in the sahasrar from the middle. The three rivers may be compared with the sympathetic, parasympathetic and central nervous systems. It is believed that with tantric practices the kundalini force rises along the susumna river toward the cerebrum.

From the logical and scientific standpoint, with the rigorous breathing exercises, complicated postures, meditation and auto suggestions our dormant genetic possibilities open up gradually and we have gradual access to the hitherto autonomic nervous systems. More and more we have command over the autonomic systems along the spinal column from coccyx to sacral, sacral to lumber and so on, our latent genetic potentials open up more fully.

From the very beginning of this awakening the tantric experiences tremendous energy and power which the ignorant person considers as supernatural. Majority of the tantrics fail after the initial achievements and because of their degeneration they cannot continue further practices properly. Their minds do not elevate in conformity with the elevation of the genetic possibilities. The most important reason is the freedom from taboos resulting in abject surrender to passions. The yogis fail because of ruthless repression of natural desires and tantrics fail because of over indulgence with these desires.

The most important hindrance is sex. Sex is the most powerful aspect of our vital force as nature demands from us in the first place that we procreate for continuation of the species. Therefore the initial success of tantric practice is accompanied by empowerment of libido and sexual capabilities and the power to attract the females into sex orgies. So most of the tantric is carried away by obsession with sex and this disables him to continue further practice successfully.

Some tantrics start making a show off of their acquired power through magic described by them as supernatural power. They attract people in large numbers to become disciples. This guru cult fulfils his greed for money and power and he loses his way.

Now his limited power cannot be enhanced through tantric practices but his greed demands more capabilities and he now resorts to fancied ideas of worship like offering sacrifices of animals and even human beings to the goddess Kali whom the superstitious and misguided tantrics consider as a blood thirsty goddess.

Chapter 12: Adventure

The tantric at the cursed plateau was a disciple of the pious tantric at Nimtala and he was at first a genius as regards tantric rituals and made rapid progress in acquiring mystic power. He had little interest in women unlike other tantrics but he was crazy about power and wanted to be the lord of this world by the grace of goddess Kali and Lord Shiva and rule over all the people of the world. Soon his greed and ego came on the path of his further progress and he asked his guru about the reason of his failure. The

guru explained to him that continued success in tantra depends on elevating the mind and to transcend the

mundane desires of money, sex and power and to get the ego dissolved into the feeling of oneness with the rest of the universe. But instead of convincing him these discourses made him dubious about the wisdom of the guru and he left the guru looking for a new wiser guru.

He soon discovered a crazy Kapalic (a vamachari tantric) and left the city with this new guru. Thereafter nobody could tell where he had gone. Now the guru had learnt from Nil that this man had settled at a lonely place on a plateau and must be engaged in some dubious practices with the hope of pleasing the goddess and acquiring enough supernatural power to rule this world. The skulls discovered by Nil and Doma indicated that he might be engaged in human sacrifice.

The guru at Nimtala had once again reminded Shyamal that Nil should move very cautiously and stop the heinous crime of his misguided disciple as early as possible. He had also pointed out that one inexplicable aspect of this misguided tantric's achievements even at the initial stage was that he could disable the powers of even his guru. No force in this world could overpower this lunatic tantric except Nil and Doma both of whom were born with divine attributes. The guru had this conviction by examining the trident mark on Nil's forehead and learning about Doma from Nil.

After reading the text several times they thought it would not be judicious to relate the tantric's background to Samten. Both agreed that their suspicions about this tantric was not unfounded. Now it was beyond doubt that the tantric had selected a desolate place forbidding entry of local people to perform goddess-worship with human sacrifice. But how could he trap the victims and from where? Moreover it appeared likely to both Nil and Doma that the water crisis was but a creation of the tantric and the story about the curse a simple hype. These new findings added new dimensions to their adventure and made them more enthusiastic to continue the exploration of the tantric's cave immediately.

They reached the shanty by the evening and after tea proceeded for the tunnel they had discovered. Further ahead along the rightward branch, the tunnel became narrow and dark because of the overhanging shrubs and creepers at the top. They dared not keep the torch switched on lest they would alert the

tantric's men. So they moved in the darkness and after some time came to the point where the track was bifurcated. Last time they had explored the left tunnel ending up in the dumping ground of remnants of human sacrifices. Now they took the right tunnel. They had to switch on the torches at times to inspect the way ahead. The tunnel turned very narrow at a place. They switched on the torches and crawled one by one out into a wider space and was elated to find the spot sloping gently on to a clear wide track which

was for sure the main track leading to the secret place of worship of the tantric. The stars above indicated that it was an open tunnel likely to be a watercourse modified into a clear path about eight feet wide. They guessed that the cave mouth they had seen on the first day was in fact constructed by the tantric. They would have to examine this whenever they got an opportunity, Nil and Doma agreed.

Now on the open track they looked carefully in all directions and then climbed down to the main

track. After they had turned the corner everything became visible as dim rays coming from the far end had illuminated the track. They got close to the wall of the track. The wall on their left was a steep rise and the other to the right inclined outward. As the path ran straight ahead they had the risk of being detected if anybody entered the track from the front side. But they had to take the risk.

Moving further ahead their nostrils were greeted with the fragrance of incense. It indicated that the place of secret worship was not far off. They thought it would be too risky to venture further because the incense indicated that the tantric might be there worshipping the goddess. They got closer to the right wall so that no body could notice them from the direction of the source of light. They soon got closer to the

spot where the tunnel had opened into a level piece of land. They cautiously peeped through the crevice of the ragged corner at the mouth of the tunnel and observed the dome like temple and the back of a red clad person. They guessed he was the tantric and he seemed to be engaged in worship of the goddess. They would have to wait at a safe place until the tantric finished his worship. Fortunately they discovered a nook, a depressed ground on the sidewall, overgrown with shrubs. After climbing up to the spot they felt safe as the place was completely engulfed in darkness so that they would be able to observe everyone in the tunnel without themselves being noticed.

An hour passed and Nil was about to doze when they heard the ringing of bells. The worship might be at the fag end, they thought. A few minutes later they heard footsteps close to the mouth of the tunnel and the entire track was illuminated brightly. Then entered the tantric with a lantern in his hand. They now got the full view of the tantric.

He was a tall lean man with large sunken eyes which had morbid brightness and ferocity that would strike any normal mind with horror.

His matted hair was neatly tied above his head. He held a trident in his left hand. His face and eyes were expressionless. After a while a group of hefty Nepalese with kurkis in their waist belts and spears in their hands closed the mouth of the tunnel with a heavy rock which they rolled up from the side of the tunnel mouth. The top of the rock rose about six feet and the inner side was smoothly polished. The guards picked up the lantern and the spears. They turned corner and the entire track in front of Nil and Doma plunged into darkness and the starry sky looked ominous. They waited for some time and then came out of the hiding. They would have to go to the other side of the rock and visit the temple and its surroundings. But it was almost impossible to scale the smooth rock and cross over to the other side. They started ruminating to device a way out.

Then they changed their plan and decided to inspect first the entrance of the tunnel at the southern end. They turned around cautiously and moved southward. The track had multiple turns. After a few turns they discovered a closed wooden gate on the right sidewall and noticed through the gaps a flight of stairs climbing steeply upward. This must be the way to the tantric's residing place up above the plateau. They moved further ahead. There were sewage drains on either side of the track which sloped gently upwards

up to some distance and then downward to the south. On their way along the track they noticed many dry courses of small springs on either side and it became clear that this track was a natural sewage for water from the plateau and the rugged hills to the east and the water course had run in two directions from the middle. They soon came to the southern end of the tunnel and found that their guess was correct. The mouth was roofed by concrete with a few walls and beams for about fifteen feet and from outside it looked exactly like the entrance of a cave. Now they once again returned to the northern end of the track and tried to devise some means to cross over to the level ground.

Doma very cautiously moved along the side of the wall grabbing the ferns hanging from the wall and Nil followed her. They eventually managed to reach the end of the track and jumped down on a cemented ground. Now they got the full view of the level piece of land. It was like a ledge jutting from the north- east corner of the plateau. It was a rectangular piece of land about forty by twenty feet. The cemented path about six feet wide ran from the mouth of the tunnel to the temple which was like an inverted U looked from the front side and about eight feet in height at the middle and five feet wide at the bottom. The wooden door of the temple was locked and on the cemented platform in front, there were two wooden altars on either side. They were clean and free from any trace of dried blood. This indicated that they were washed clean after every sacrifice. They rounded the temple along the oblong portico. The temple had tapered down from its roof and the slopes of the hill behind was strewn with remnants of burnt trees overgrown with creepers and shrubs. On the opposite side the rise of the plateau was also scattered with burnt trunks. The hills down the western side were steep and covered with pine saplings.

They reached the eastern end of the ground and guessed that they could reach their approach track by grabbing the burnt trunks of the trees. The moon was now up in the clear sky and everything was clearly visible. They climbed down the slope and soon reached the spot close to the mouth of the tunnel they had come along. So they could reach the temple taking a shorter path and with less effort.

The new moon night was only a few days ahead and they decided to undertake the next venture on that day. They now had an idea about the worship time of the tantric. But he might take a longer time on the new moon night. But they could wait till the worship was complete. They should come early and hide behind the slope behind the temple taking cover of the burnt trunks and shrubs.

Nil consulted Doma how to break off the strong lock at the door of the temple. He at this place cannot get access to acetylene lamps.

The huge lock was too strong and could not be opened with iron nails. Any effort to break it with stones would create sharp noise and alert the tantric and his men. So, they would have to visit the temple once again before their final venture and find if the rings holding the lock could be opened. They also thought of the alternative of entering into the temple from the hind side. They had already seen loosely fitted wooden slabs at the back of the temple. Anyway, no further decision could be taken unless they scrutinized the temple once again.

They were now too tired and it was almost dawn. They also felt hungry and took some dried fruits. They fell asleep as soon as they touched bed and woke late in the next morning.

Chapter 13: The Tantric's Trap

Next evening they took the short cut and climbed up to the eastern end of the temple compound early. They peeped into the ground and were surprised to find nobody in or around the temple. Still they did not take risk. They waded along the curvy side of the hill and reached their selected hiding spot behind the temple. They tore creepers and thrashed down bushes to make a suitable nook. They guessed that it was not yet time for the tantric to start his worship. They waited for a long time occasionally climbing up to

the edge of the hill and peeping into the level ground. The mouth of the southern track was still closed with the rock. They waited patiently and when the time at which the tantric had departed the day before was past. it seemed to them that the tantric had some specific schedule of worship and it was not a worship day. So they decided to climb up and inspect the temple. If there was any sign of movement at the mouth of the track they could get back to the hiding. The moon was yet to rise and cover of darkness would also help them to remain undetected. They cautiously climbed up and roamed across the entire ground and there was no sign of anybody.

They waited for about an hour more and then approached the temple. Nil closely examined the rings connecting the lock. One of the rings was rusted and became thinner at its attachment with the wooden door. This could easily be loosened with the help of an iron rod. He turned around to tell Doma that they should return now and come on the new moon night with the necessary contrivances. But his heart got

into sudden flutter as he heard the grave voice uttering in distinct Bengali, 'I knew you would come again. Yester night you left your foot marks while you had trespassed. So I've set this trap to befool you and capture you. Mother Kali has sent you to get my last 'bali' (sacrifice) completed and the crucial night is only two days ahead.'

Nil soon regained his composure, exchanged glances with Doma and both of them rushed toward the eastern end. The raucous laughter of the tantric echoed in the hills and he uttered in a menacing voice,

'fools you cannot escape from me.' He raised his hand and Nil and Doma found themselves tied closely by a red ribbon from waist upward, hands fitted tight with their bodies. They could not make any movement as both of them were tied closely together. The tantric now laughed again and said, 'my men would soon lock both of you in a room and keep you confined till the grand puza on new moon night. Boy you'll be

my tenth and last bali as I had promised to the goddess. Oh, after this bali I would get the supreme blessings of mother Kali and become invincible in this world.'

He looked at Doma scornfully and said in the local dialect, 'you look like a girl from the Lepcha village and you seem to be spying on this sacred place with your Bengali lover. Now your lover would be sacrificed to the goddess. And how should I punish you for your grave sin? You've done me great favor

by presenting me this boy for bali. So. I'd spare you torturous death. Your punishment would be very light. I'd gift you to my men for sex-game.' The tantric started laughing again frantically.

Neither Nil nor Doma could utter a single word. Thought of the horrible fate benumbed their senses. All of a sudden Nil felt a tickling sensation in his coccyx as though some insect had been moving slowly up his spine. The sensation became intensified as it moved up and the heat coursing through his whole body was unendurable. Then all of a sudden flashes of lightning emerged out of his forehead which mingled with similar flashes from the forehead of Doma. In a moment the magic ribbon binding them disappeared. The tantric looked awe stricken. He raised his hand again and made a desperate effort but nothing happened. Nil and Doma realized that some uncanny force had robbed the tantric of his tanra power. In desperation the tantric tried to raise the trident lying in front of him but he was now too weak to lift it. He trembled in rage and started calling out his men for help in a meek voice.

Nil and Doma exchanged glances and dashed toward the hillside. They realized that mystic power of the tantric could no longer do them any harm but the hefty Nepalese could physically overpower them. They got to the edge of the ground and started scaling down like squirrels. They would have to reach the escape route before the men of the tantric could get at them.

They eventually reached the end of the rise and got closer to the clear track they had made. The last part was a cluster of burnt tree trunks arranged in rows making a tunnel like opening. They entered the narrow opening and Doma instructed Nil to race down at his best as soon as he reached the clear track. They got ready as the sprinters do before the whistle blares. They looked up and cold waves raced down their spines as they found Namsel blocking their escape route brandishing a vast kurki (a very powerful chopper like weapon used mainly by the Nepalese).

Chapter 14: Bhutia Riddle

They stood motionless and watched the gigantic Bhutia with the sharp weapon standing in front of them like a demon. It would be sheer folly to try to trick this man, especially because of the weapon the single strike of which might cut off a man into two. Both Nil and Doma realized that they would have to surrender meekly and this Bhutia would then produce them before the notorious tantric. Chill streamed down Nil's spine to think about his fate, being sacrificed to goddess Kali like a helpless goat. He could think no more.

Namsell remained stand still, expressionless as if he was a lifeless zombie. Then to their surprise his face creased into a mild smile and it appeared affable. The smile intensified before bemused Nil and Doma and then the man burst out into loud laughter.

'Young boy and girl, you seem to be worried and in haste. Anything happened up there?' Namsell queried in a friendly tone.

His attitude seemed friendly. These hill people cannot conceal their evil intensions unlike the crooked plains people. Both Nil and Doma now felt relieved and they related what had just happened.

Namsell heaved a sigh of relief and said in an ecstatic tone, 'the notorious tantric has now lost all his powers. You have done what you'd been entrusted with by god. Now get away from this place without wasting time. The tantric's men must be in the lookout for you. Drive straight to the caves without waiting at your shanti.'

Namsell's words seemed unreal to them. They got befuddled and stood motionless.

'Move on without delay. His men are not far off.' Namsell said in a commanding tone.

Nil and Doma jumped out of the tunnel into the clear track and started dashing down recklessly. They did not stop at the shanti and made right for the caves. Reaching the caves Nil fell down unconscious. When his senses returned he felt pain all over his body. Doma and

Samten were seated alongside his bedstead. As soon as Nil opened his eyes Samten asked him to open his mouth and he dropped a herbal powder on Nil's tongue. It worked like magic and Nil felt his energy reviving. Then his mind got obsessed with Namsell. Who was this man, why was he spying on them and why did he give them opportunity to escape from the clutches of the tantric? He could not be the tantric's man. Did he then belong to a rival group? Nil could not make out anything. Doma and Samten too were in the dark about the mysterious behavior of Namsell.

Nil wanted to have some talk with Shyamal. Reaching for his cell phone he found an sms. It was from Shyamal. He was coming to the caves very soon. Nil should wait there until he arrived. Nil got completely puzzled. For what purpose was Shyamal coming to this remote place? Nil could not make out anything and gave up thinking after confused speculations.

The cell phone rang again to indicate receipt of another sms. It could be some advertisement he thought. He had almost deleted the message when he noticed the name of Rita. This was another surprise for him. She too was accompanying Shyamal.

Nil's head got jumbled as he could not make out anything of what had happened since they were detected by the tantric. Every incident appeared inconsistent and unreal and he thought it could be simply a dream. Samten confirmed that he too had got information that Shyamal and a Bengali lady was coming to this place and they had asked by a messenger to arrange for their travel from South Sikkim.

Chapter 15: Shyamal's Story

A few days later Shyamal and Rita were accompanied to the caves by Sangey. They had come via Namche of South Sikkim. The route was less difficult than one via Manebhanjan and the part they had to go on foot was a gentle climb down of about six kilometers. Rita in a deep blue sari looked gorgeous. She greeted Nil ebulliently and Doma devoured her with burning eyes.

Nil said to Shyamal, 'I'm really befuddled and can't understand anything. Will you please explain the reason of your mystic visit?'

'It's a long story. We are tired now and hungry too. I'll disclose everything after lunch and some rest.'

Sangey led them to the dining enclave. Doma looked gloomy and started casting occasional hateful glances at Rita. 'She must be aggrieved and jealous about Rita', Nil thought and taking Doma aside said,

'believe me, there had never been anything between me and this lady.'

'But her looks tell some different story.'

'It's a mistake on your part. Plains people are different from hill people and they are crooked. You cannot understand their intentions from their outward behavior. Most of the aristocrat ladies behave this way as though she has fallen in love with the person she is talking with.'

'Still my instinct hints me she has something about you in her mind., although I believed you are innocent. So be cautious about this lady. Moreover, I can't understand what purpose they have come here for? Do you know anything?'

'Me too is completely in the dark. But my friend assured me he would disclose everything after lunch and some rest.'

'Okay let's wait till then.'

There was more surprise stored for them. Shyamal and Rita slept for about an hour after lunch. Thereafter they were summoned by

Samten to his cave. Nil, Doma and Sangey too congregated in the cave. All of them assembled around Shyamal and Samten. Shyamal was going to start his story but he was interrupted by the sudden entrance of Namsell which startled both Nil and Doma. Namsell saluted Shyamal and said,

'Everything okay sir.'

He turned around and greeted Nil and Doma with a naughty smile. Nil was now completely flummoxed. Looking at his bewildered countenance, Shyamal smiled and said,

'it's quite natural for you to be befuddled. Namsell is an inspector of Sikkim secret service.'

'Then you and Mrs. Sen?'

'We are both in secret service from the IPS (Indian Police Service) cadre. My job at the agro- corporation was a lie and Mrs. Sen's job at Mitra's office is a special arrangement for cover to facilitate our investigations.'

'Sir, everything is okay and in accordance with your directions. All the escape routes have been blocked by police and commandoes. Now we are waiting for your signal to initiate Operation Tantric', Namsell interrupted.

'Go back to the spot and wait for my final signal' Namsel left and Shyamal resumed his story.

'A few years ago Nepal police sought help of Indian police regarding disappearance of children from villages adjacent to India. They suspected that the child lifters sneaked from India to Nepal and after the mischief escaped to Indian territories beyond the jurisdiction of Nepal police. I was then entrusted with the task of investigating the matter. Mrs. Sen was appointed my chief assistant. I soon learnt from informers in the hills that a tantric from Tarapith had settled at the summit of a hill and was engaged in esoteric tantra practices. My doubt immediately fell on the tantric and I suspected human sacrifice. There was an educational institute in the hills run by Mr. Mitra who had at first joined the West Bengal Police as a Deputy Superintend of Police but resigned to look after his family business after his father's death. I contacted him and sought his help and he accepted my proposal to accept Mrs. Sen as an employee to give her cover while investigating the mischief. This cover gave her opportunity to gather important

information through the institution of their firm in the hills. She soon informed me of Inspector Namsell of the Sikkim Secret Service.'

'He looks like a rustic Bhutia!' Nil uttered in surprise.

'Yes and this is his advantage. His father is a rich businessman, a transport operator at Sikkim and Darjeeling. Namsell graduated from Darjeeling Govt. college and thereafter joined Sikkim secret service. Anyway, I contacted Namsell. He accepted my offer very enthusiastically. His family had a tantric tradition and so he was entrusted with the task of collecting full information about the activities of the tantric under the guise of a disciple. I knew fully well that it would not be judicious to undertake searching in the tantric's den simply on guesswork. If he is proved innocent, there would be religious reaction and the govt. would take punitive actions against us for hurting religious sentiments of common people without any reason.

In the meantime my wife gave an important information that her guru knew the tantric in the hills and the account of her guru substantiated my view that the tantric was connected with the child lifting mischief.'

'Then it is you who had directed Namsell to trail me!' Nil said and laughed. Everybody except the grave Samten joined the laughter.

'Mr. Banerjee you'd panicked Nil to hell!' Rita's sharp giggle filled the entire cave and Doma glanced at her with burning eyes.

'You're absolutely right', Shyamal continued, 'I'll come to it soon but let me first relate what happened to Namsell's investigations. He tried his best but was not permitted to meet the tantric under the ruse that he was a Buddhist. So we had no way to learn what was going on inside the tantric's den. Then like a gift from heaven I came upon Nil after a long time and learnt that he was going to assist the

Lepchas to resolve their problem in which the tantric had some hand for sure. I had no idea about his divine power and was therefore concerned about his safety. So I directed Namsell to remain close to Nil ever since he had reached New Jalpaiguri. His guess was correct. The Bhutia he'd come upon at various places was none but Namsell.'

Shyamal paused for a while and asked for a glass of water. Samten called an attendant and asked him for water and also to prepare spice tea for all of them.

'Has Sangey too something to do with the police?' Nil asked.

'No Mr. Roy I'm still a journalist', Sangey said with an affable smile. Nil turned toward Rita and said, 'surprise! When did you join the IPS?'

Rita swung her body voluptuously and said, 'one year after your resignation the president of the governing body of the college humiliated me over a trifling mistake and I immediately resigned. You know what a nasty person he is. He poses to be an academician but he does not have the minimum sense of etiquette. After resignation I decided to appear at the IPS examination and I came out successful. Mr. Banerjee, although younger in age than me, had joined the IPS much earlier and he is a senior officer.'

Doma looked utterly chagrined and said glumly, 'I've nothing to do here until Mr. Banerjee resumes his story. Let me go and look after tea.'

Doma left like an angry teenage girl and this sent Nil out of wits. He could no longer continue conversation with Rita with ease. Rita too became gloomy and silent. 'It is very difficult to understand the female mind', Nil thought. He realized that he would never be able to alley Doma's jealousy and hatred for Rita.

After tea Shyamal resumed his narration, 'I'd earlier talked with Namsell and asked him to find some alternative to collect information about the tantric's activities in the hills. He informed me that the tantric had supernatural power and feared by local people. This was the reason he failed to find an informer from among the local people. The guru of my wife also subscribed to the belief about mystic power of the tantric. Now learning about Nil, Namsell collected information from the Lepcha village and assured me that he was the right person to nullify the power of the tantric. Namsell had already heard about the divine power of the Lepcha girl. He got confirmed about Nil's divine power when he noticed the trident mark on his forehead at their first encounter at New Jalpaiguri. I myself had little faith in these. But still I had the hunch that with Nil's help alone I'd be able to resolve the tantric mystery. So I directed Namsell to assist Nil and the Lepcha girl by all possible means. Now the tantric is almost in our hands. But we are to wait and see. There's many a slip between the cup and the lip.'

'But what makes you so confident about the mischief of the tantric?' Nil queried

'The urgent message from Namsell had confirmed me. Following your track he too had discovered the dumping ground for skulls and human skeletons. Moreover, when the tantric conversed with you before your final showdown Namsell recorded the conversation and also video-photographed your encounter by remote control device and this would be our evidence in the law court.'

Shyamal laughed and everybody joined him and Samten got busy making arrangements for the night stay of Shyamal and Rita. The attendant informed that dinner was ready.

Chapter 16: Operation Tantric

Next morning when Nil woke up he learnt from Shyamal that Rita had left on an important secret assignment and she could not wait for the operation. Namsell had accompanied her to the vehicle point.

Nil thought it had something to do with Doma who now looked ecstatic and there was no trace of the gloom that took possession of her the day before. Shyamal handed Nil a note from Rita. It was very brief.

'Be happy with the hill girl. She loves you deeply and would be a good wife. Your happiness is my happiness but I hope you'd have the grace to recognize the love of this poor lady.'

Nil remained silent for a long time. Doma certainly loved him and he too loved her, but could this love be ended in marriage or they too would have to live in lifelong loneliness like Rita?

The operation took only a few hours. The tantric looked very sick and he was sent to a hospital at Siliguri under strict commando guard. All his men were arrested and these Nepalese fell at the feet of Nil and Doma, whom they believed to be incarnates of Lord Shiva and goddess Parvati, and begged for mercy. They confessed everything and this was recorded by Shyamal.

Shyamal, Nil, Doma, Namsell and Sangey reached the top of the plateau and joined a military engineer and his men. They now were led by the engineer to a spot farther to the north east. A sluice gate blocking the rivulet to the Lepcha village came to their view. The engineer explained that with this sluice gate the tantric had diverted water of the channel to a tributary of the River Tista at Sikkim.

The tantric knew well that the agriculture-dependent Lepchas would seek his help as soon as they were deprived of irrigation water and it would be easier for him to get men from the Lepcha village for child lifting at Nepal. In fact this was the secret job of the Lepcha laborers who were sent to the tantric in exchange for temporary resumption of flow of water in the rivulet.

'But what about the extra terrestrial vehicle and the conflagration?' Nil asked.

'It too was a handiwork of the tantric.' Shyamal continued, 'the arrested Nepalese have confessed that by direction of the tantric they had exploded high power crackers on the plateau that set fire on the trees spread with petrol.'

'But what about the other alien vehicles observed by the elderly Lepchas?'

'I can't say anything about them. I've my own ideas but it would be injudicious to make any comment that may hurt the sentiments of the simple Lepchas.'

The men of the engineer got busy fixing dynamite explosives at different corners of the sluice gate. Then a coil of electric wire was fitted into the explosive devices. Following the course of the dry channel the engineer and his men started moving downwards uncoiling the wire. Shyamal and his team followed him. Reaching a safe distance they came out of the channel bed to a level piece of land. The ends of the wires were fitted to a battery. The Nepali engineer then came to Nil and Doma, and offered them pranam which embarrassed both of them. Then he said,

'divine beings, accept my respect and have the grace to switch on the detonator.'

He led Nil and Doma to the device and as directed by the engineer's men they rested their right thumbs side by side and presses the button. A horrible rumbling shook the hills and flames and rains of stones were visible in the northern sky. Then the blasting sound was drowned by roaring of rushing water. All of them climbed to a higher place and soon they observed the tidal wave like downward flow of water along the rivulet. Nil and Doma grabbed each other's arms and dived into the roaring and raging water before the bewildered eyes of everybody. Soon they looked like tiny dots bobbing up and down the raging current and then disappeared behind the hills.

About the Author

The author of this volume Dr. Ratan Lal Basu is a Ph. D. in Economics (on Arthaśāstra, the treatise on political economy and statecraft composed by a Brāhmaṇa scholar Kauṭilya around 300 B. C.). He retired as principal from a Government-Sponsored College at Kolkata, and after retirement got fully occupied with research and publishing activities pertaining to Indology, ancient economics, modern economic problems, economic history, yoga and tantra cult, statecraft, international relations and espionage, ethics and morality and also fiction in English and Bengali (his mother tongue).